Of Crimson Joy

by erAto

Alumbra Publishing

2019

Of Crimson Joy
part of the *Regency Romantics*,
© 2017 Talia Felix

Reprinted by
Alumbra Publishing
2019

978-1-7341846-0-0

Year:

1810

CHAPTER 1

Sir Howard Rowereigh, 2nd Baronet was from a family which had not been Sirs for very long; nor for that matter had they been Rowereighs for long. Both features had been bestowed within his own lifetime, as a consideration from a powerful friend; before, the family name had been Grimesby. The Grimesby family had owned some farmland for several generations, and by the middle of the 18th century a funny thing had taken place: this land had become very valuable, not for the land itself, but for the ten men eligible to vote who happened to dwell upon it. Reginald Grimesby, father to Howard, had realized that these ten voters were of considerable merit.

It had fallen that the Grimesby property, a little hillside known as Goseth Tree (just what was a "Goseth" was a mystery lost to all time), had several hundred years before been considered a booming and bustling city center. A few ruinous houses inhabited mostly by ants, and a mossy shell that had once been a grand abbey, attested to the site's former glory. Despite what changes the Reformation had brought to the region, the city of Goseth Tree had been recorded on the books as an important city and duly granted the power of choosing two elected burgesses to serve as members of Parliament.

As the choice of these two members of Parliament was in the hands of the ten voters, it was little trouble for Reginald Grimesby to threaten to evict any tenants disinclined to vote in a desirable way — this being of course the way that *he* desired. This phenomenon had been noted by some wealthy men with aspirations, who began bribing Mr. Grimesby to favor their being elected to the non-city's coveted positions. Grimesby was only too happy to oblige them.

At length, Mr. Grimesby had sold the property at Goseth Tree outright, in return for a goodly sum and the title of a Baronet, which his new friends were well in the position to bestow him. The delighted Reginald Grimesby commemorated the event by purchasing the historic Rowereigh Castle in Yorkshire, a name which did too much honor to the ancient wreck of a building, although the family started at once in making renovations to turn the dismal stone structure into a bearable dwelling. Now with a title and a castle, Grimesby renamed himself Rowereigh after the property he owned. Upon Reginald's death, many years later, the title of Baronet Rowereigh was passed down to his only son, Howard.

Howard had been lucky in birth, lucky in speculation, and some would argue he had been lucky in love — for it would later be said by Tennyson, "'Tis better to have loved and lost, than never to have loved at all." His first wife, Laura, had been a perfect match for him. They were both twenty years old when they married; but he was made a widower at twenty-two. The short marriage had been pure joy to young Howard, and he was very eager to remarry and to regain that joy which he had lost. In a few years he had wed again to a woman who, on paper, would have seemed every bit as merry a match for him as Laura, but in actual practice Howard did not find nearly so pleasing — perhaps because she still was not Laura, and never had possessed Laura's joyous nature or pleasing quirks. After thirteen years, Frances, the second wife, died of what nobody at all suspected to be poison, and Sir Howard was left again to look for love and happiness. Happiness, indeed, was more desired and more elusive than ever for him; as it was, Sir Howard's slow-poison technique had — deservedly — backfired, for all the time he had been dosing his wife, he himself had experienced many accidental self-doses and cross-contaminations, which in the end had left him with irreversible digestive troubles. Medicating himself with laudanum and undergoing frequent bloodlettings seemed to be all that provided any relief.

Indeed, the medical men in all their wisdom had allotted Sir Howard health enough to succeed in courting a maiden of half his age, named Agnes Summersby. She was of a fairly good family — in fact, her own father, Sir William, was a fellow Baronet, and had a lengthier claim to the title. Unlike Sir Howard, however, Sir William was not lucky in money or finances. Summersby Manor had been let and every property not in entail was sold off long ago to escape an alternative of debtor's prison, and by careful living and very frugal manners which dared the lines of respectability, the family's money had lasted the family into Agnes's reaching a marriageable age. She was the only surviving child of the Summersby house, and her parents had made it known that she was expected to marry well, or be lost, for there was no hope of supporting her in any comfort as a spinster or a wife of a poor man. Her father had even been so uncouth as to put it into such simple terms, from time to time.

For her own part, Agnes was not one of those fresh young women who had dreams of anything greater than a prosperous marriage, and was unbothered by the urgings of her parents toward one — for Agnes took a great pride in her role as a dutiful daughter. The teachings of her church, and of the favored literature of the day, taught her there was nothing more virtuous than taking up such a role. Duty to one's parents was in the Ten Commandments, was it not? And then, once advanced to wifedom, her obligations would be to the wishes of her husband and any other members of the family which might come into creation. She was perfectly contented with these thoughts, and eagerly awaited her ability to fulfill them. A virtuous life of submission and obedience was all that she longed for. When fulfilling the wants of others is the pleasure of one's life, it seemed to her, all life should be a pleasure; for others are never lacking in wants. This was the fantasy she had for herself: a happy life as a capable and dutiful wife and mother, bringing joy to everyone.

At age 21 and knowing she was unlikely to get any better proposals, the attentions of her father's friend were welcomed enough, her own parents seemed to approve, Sir Howard succeeded well enough at concealing his medical disorders in her presence, and no one ever suspected the real cause of the death of the second Lady Rowereigh. Taken all together, what objection was there? Sir Howard was wealthy, established, fond of her. There was not the slightest objection from anybody when at last he requested the honor of receiving her hand in marriage. A long engagement was not necessary to the couple; the wedding was planned for a month from the day of the agreement. Invitations were sent, feasts prepared, and Agnes invested in some new shoes and a new turban-style headcap decked with plumes, for the occasion. Her favorite silver satin gown would suffice for the dress.

The night before the wedding, Agnes's two dearest friends stayed the night at her house. These were Antonia Bennet and Elizabeth Perkins, both of whom she had known since early childhood, even before her brief period of formal schooling from ages 10 to 12, which had been all that her parents could afford for her. Both Antonia and Elizabeth were engaged to be married, but of the longtime trio, Agnes was the first to really *be* wed — and that she should be the first, was no shock to her dear friends, who knew full well her good nature and virtuous ways. They were happy for her and her good fortune in finding so desirable a match, even if the bridegroom's age was nearer to her father's than to her own.

As the girls rolled and braided their hair in advance of the important day, hoping to have perfect curls set in by the next morning, they chattered excitedly about all their future plans and the coming events.

"Have you been given any time alone with him yet?" asked Antonia, hinting meaningfully at something.

"Not at all, but for the proposal," said Agnes, endeavoring not to seem shocked.

"There will be time enough for that tomorrow," said Antonia; and a mutual blush formed upon the faces of all three girls as loose visions of the sexual scene were picturized in their minds.

"You will surely have at least fourteen children," joked Elizabeth.

"All boys," added Antonia.

Agnes doused her hair in a few splashes of cologne, hoping it would help to set it. The cooling rosemary-citrus scent helped to calm her nerves. She let a laugh sputter forth at these considerations which she had left unimagined till this time, and which her friends now were joking upon. It was no mark against them, she supposed, to bring up something that naturally should become part of her life from this point on. But no matter — it was all part of her duty. She would endure it.

The sun had barely cracked the horizon when Agnes rose from her bed and began her preparations for the big day. Her wedding day. The date was March 31st, 1810. Would it change her? Would she still be the same old Agnes Summersby — even after she became Lady Howard Rowereigh? The first thing that struck was how, due to her family's poverty, she had never had servants to help dress her — only an all-purpose maid ever served with the family, a loyal old lady who answered to the name of Ginny, and who spent most of her time doing laundry and chopping firewood with quite more skill than one would have expected. But to Agnes, any necessary assistance with dressing usually came from her mother or from some friend who was joining her in preparation. Yet surely a man like Sir Howard would have many servants, and supply her with a personal chambermaid, maybe even a private hairdresser...? But these mysteries would be solved at a later time. She would be ready for whatever was ahead. Quite ready, and willing. Willing to take whatever her husband and master was to give her, for good or bad. This was now to be her life, for good and all.

Her friends and parents were risen from slumber all about the same time as the bride-to-be. They helped her to dress. Antonia and Elizabeth were from good families; but their friendship was so longstanding that they'd never really seen anything odd in Agnes's living conditions or financial state, until relatively recently in life. Even then, they perceived no wrong in it — and now here she was, marrying a rich Baronet that any woman of their station would claim if but given the chance. This was surely her patience and good behavior being rewarded by some higher power, and should be held up as an example to women everywhere of the rewards to be had from virtue.

With everyone dressed in their finest clothing, the company herded together in a rented coach and bounced their way to the appointed church, which was the Summersby family's own local parish, a little Norman relic overcrowded inside with dead people's memorials. Agnes was far too familiar with these dead to be distressed by their presence at her wedding; their markers had been a part of her life so long that to have them there was like an extension of the wedding guests. The medieval brass cutout of Sir Richard Hartelwyde and the century old marble bust of Dorothea Bartleby, the worn stone on the floor for John Kensing, the plain plaque on the wall for Ebenezer Mitcham, were all like family themselves.

The wedding to Sir Howard was perfect in every respect. Friends and family wept appropriately, the bride blushed and bloomed, the groom looked respectable and cheerful at his own good fortune in gaining such a lovely thing for a wife. The service from the Book of Common Prayer was read without excess retardation. A fine ring of gold and silver was slid upon the waiting finger of Agnes, and the couple with their attending friends went off to the breakfast which awaited them.

The mirth and perfection did not last long. Already at the breakfast, Sir Howard was beginning to feel very unwell. There was some initial thought that it was merely due to excess drink, but he had in fact been perfectly cautious with his intake. He put it off to the richness of the food and did what he could to control the desires of his body to expel the victuals back out, from one end of his body or the other. Bride and groom left early, and the wedding night was spent with Agnes and the servants nursing Sir Howard, preparing poultices and herbal tonics and emptying chamberpots till the wee hours, when at last the sick man succeeded in falling asleep. Agnes was a bit disappointed but also a bit relieved in the turn of events; for anxious as she was to consummate the union, her heart still quaked with a nervous fear whenever she thought about it.

Sadly for Agnes, her situation was not much to improve after this. Her married life continued being channeled through an unlucky route. Sir Howard's health seemed only to worsen, and his usual doses of laudanum were no longer proving adequate to ease his gastro-intestinal unhappiness; his doses were increased, but to the detriment of his personality. He was no longer the bright, charming, affectionate being who once had courted her; he had become dull, grumpy and more fond of his weak broths and gruels than of her. He tended to stink of either vomit or feces at any time. The new bride had no availability for making calling cards with her married name, paying visits to old friends, nor buying new matronly gowns — her every moment belonged to Howard Rowereigh, not as a beloved wife but as a nursemaid.

Trying to make the best of it all, Agnes took pride in her dutiful attendance upon her husband, staying by his side for hours hoping her mere presence might do him good; or when that seemed all too hopeless, she involved herself with helping the servants with the washings and feedings and dosing of medicines. When the barber would come to shave Sir Howard and let some of his blood, it was Agnes herself who emptied the blood-dish into the trash heap hidden behind the weathered stone walls, then carefully scrubbed the dish with water and soap to await its next use.

The good feelings of doing the right thing and leading a dutiful, subservient life could only carry Agnes so far, however. Her spirits began to suffer, her cheerful bloom began to fade, the sleepless nights began to influence her mind, and her overwork began to transform her features. No cologne or burnt perfume could really conceal the stench around her husband and his personal items, and in time the bad air of it started to have some detrimental effect on the health of Agnes herself.

CHAPTER 2

When Agnes's parents came for their first visit to the newlyweds, four months after the ceremony, they were so aghast at the change in their daughter that they insisted she should come with them immediately to the nearest spa, to get her health back. Agnes refused, asserting that it was her duty to attend to her husband, and she could not be swayed by any argument, no matter how well-reasoned.

The Summersbys had known from Agnes's letters that her husband had not been doing well, but they did not picture just how poor a condition it had become, nor how it had wretchedly altered Agnes herself. Sir William having no desire to see his daughter set up in a life of prosperity and status only to be drained and buried within months of gaining it, went to Sir Howard directly, to appeal to him. The sick man's bedchamber stank so violently that Sir William was forced to hold a handkerchief perfumed with Hungary Water to his face as he spoke.

"Agnes is unfailing in her duties to you," argued Sir William to the sick man, "She will not leave your side even for her own sake. Yet the sudden change in her condition is undeniable. It would be for the best, do you not think, if she were to leave for a few weeks to recover herself, before returning to you?"

Sir Howard's opium-laden and blood-drained reply was some form of grumbling which perhaps did contain words, though not of any good English. Sir William was left to assume it had not been in complete agreement with his wishes, and so he began anew:

"A trip to the spa would perhaps be of benefit not just to Agnes, but to the both of you. The healing waters have been known to affect many a cure. Harrogate is not a far journey from here, and the both of you might gain well by it. Why, old friend, if you were cured, it would surely be a double happiness to me — and Agnes too would gain a double happiness in the cure of her own health problems, and in seeing her husband well again. Surely you value your own health as much as anyone? Would not a trip to take the waters be a worthy investment of time and trouble?"

Similar solicitations eventually produced from the inebriated Sir Howard murmurs and mumbles which appeared to be in agreement, and Sir William went at once to notify the staff and his daughter of the decision. Though to meddle in the household of his daughter's husband might normally be importune, it seemed to Sir William that under the circumstances which he had witnessed, of a brand-new bride and an incapacitated husband, some outside help was to be necessary to get the marriage off on a good footing.

The Summersbys cut their visit short only after they were quite certain that their daughter's trip to Harrogate was underway. They departed in the morning and, a few hours later, Agnes and Sir

Howard were taken in their private coach, along with packed belongings and a good supply of medical necessities to tide them through the journey. Harrogate was about 30 hours' gentle ride from their home, which required two overnight stays in small villages before arriving at the town, to the fashionable inn where they were to stay for their recovery. A pump room was located inside the building, with attendants dispensing glasses of the sulfur-water, and in the cellar of the inn there was a bath for visitors to soak themselves. The famous "stinking" waters were highly regarded, and certainly to Agnes after her troubles, the scent was nowhere near as unpleasant as what she was used to enduring in her own home.

The windows of their room were opened to allow in the fresh, revivifying air of the village; the servants unpacked the trunks, and the married couple hurried downstairs, where they changed into long gowns to wear in the water. The bathing rooms were dimly lit — but that was not wholly unwelcome, as the waters tended to render the cotton gowns transparent, and one was not guaranteed complete privacy. The tubs were fashioned like miniature swimming pools, with a shallow and deep end cut into the stone floors, and a channel going along back which filled them all with the natural mineral water. The tubs were encased in stalls to offer some privacy to the bathers as they lay soaking. A servant girl waited by the door with dry towels and sheets.

Immersed up to the collarbone, Agnes kneeled in her tub and seemed to feel at once the rejuvenating effect upon her tired skin. Bathers through the ages have known that something about bath water has a curious effect upon the mind, and at once it sent hers into a thoughtful contemplation. She realized that this little moment to herself — even if Howard was deposited in the next tub over — was the first time in four months that she had actually felt *good*. Not good like the proper pride of a duty well carried out, but an actual moment of feeling like she was well and had nothing in the world to worry about, like her skin was cozy instead of dry or unclean, like her mind was unburdened, like her body was comfortable. It was the first time she had felt *happy*.

Meanwhile, Sir Howard was finding his soak a bit less pleasant — the heat was disagreeable to him, and seemed to be making him lightheaded and dizzy. He remained in the tub for as long as he could withstand, but within a few minutes determined that he could not abide it further, and red-faced and exhausted, he went back to his rooms. Agnes was left to stay put.

So far, Agnes had done her duty in attending to the happiness of her husband. She had expected that such an activity would prove equally fulfilling to herself, but she was coming to realize that it was not, in fact, what she had been intending when she agreed to the union. Instead of fulfillment, she was feeling ragged, useless and wretched. She received no affection from her dear husband, and was eternally left in doubt and dread whether it was something the matter with her that provoked his disinterest. And this, she now realized, was the future she had signed up for.

But perhaps all hope was not lost. Earnestly, she wished that the healing waters of Harrogate would provide a perfect cure to her husband, and from there they could start afresh upon the happy married life she had envisioned for herself — helping her husband manage the house and keep finances and look after children, attend to his appearance, plan dinners and entertain guests — that was the life she had pictured. A life full of love, done for the honor and happiness of her husband, but still, a life more vivid and fulfilling than what she was now getting in caring for a sickly, revolting man whose illness was draining the life out of both of them.

Alas, a month of sulfur-water offered little effect upon the health of Sir Howard Rowereigh. His sensitive stomach was too badly injured for the Harrogate waters to be of any good. The local medics were not better than his personal physicians, but it came to pass that one of the doctors suggested the strong water of Harrogate was perhaps not suitable to his particular condition, and that the milder waters to be found at Bath would hold a better effect for him. Bath being a considerable distance from them, the news was not welcomed by Sir Howard, who frankly did not have much faith in the water-cure at all. On the other hand, Agnes had shown notable improvement with the Harrogate waters, and thus was convinced utterly of their curative properties. When she learned of the doctor's recommendation, she became insistent to her husband that they ought to depart for Bath at once.

"Nothing would delight me more, than to see my husband returned to health," she coaxed. "There is certainly no financial reasoning to refrain from it — it might be a few days of travel, which is uncomfortable to be sure, but what price is that if there should be a cure for you at the end of the road?" She continued to urge him and argue for all the wonderful reasons to make the trip, and finally in a moment when the laudanum haze was adequately weak, he gave way to her pleas. The couple began to make arrangements to travel to Bath at once. The bags were packed, the horses readied, and at dawn the next day they departed. Upon the rural roads, muddied by the seasonal rains, it would take most of a week, they estimated, to reach the city of Bath.

On the second day of travel, Sir Howard's illness became too severe for him to continue. His intestines wouldn't hold, his stomach wouldn't hold — vomit and diarrhea were all over the interior of the coach and on his poor long-suffering wife. It was suggested by the servants that as the couple were not so far from their own home, they ought to return there; but Agnes was aghast at the idea, and could instantly see her dreams of a cured husband slipping away.

"Oh, but we must get him to Bath! His very life may depend upon it!" she protested. When it was argued that Sir Howard was in no condition to travel, tears were brought to her eyes.

Agnes's condition was not lost on the servants; they too had witnessed how her health and good spirits faded in her husband's home, and also had witnessed the improvements that the healing waters had effected upon her. Helpfully, Sir Howard's valet, David, suggested that while Sir Howard was certainly in no condition to travel at present, there was no reason Agnes shouldn't continue onward for her own sake — her health was in jeopardy as well, and would surely be bettered by the waters at Bath. Sir Howard doubtless would follow her once his health was permitting; he could hire a coach to make the trip when he was ready. Incoherent murmurs from Sir Howard were interpreted as agreement to the wisdom of David's plan, and Agnes was left with the final say on the matter.

The thought of leaving her husband distressed her, but the thought that her husband soon would be joining her did ease the concern.

She imagined she might be able to prepare their lodgings to his comfort and satisfaction in advance of his arrival, and that they could live in some comfort whilst the cure was undertaken. Then at last she would be able to see her husband happy and healthy again.

Agnes agreed. A diversion was made back to their own home, where the trunks and luggage were sorted and separated, and Sir Howard was taken away to his own bed. The coach was given a fast cleaning and the cushions removed from inside. Without bothering to stay for any further rest or recuperation, Agnes and her luggage were packed back into the coach, her maid, Fanny, taken in company, and the coachman hurried them off in the direction of Bath without any more delay.

CHAPTER 3

Viscount Lionel Winthrope was descended from both English and German aristocratic lines. Now 30 years old, the blondeness of his hair maintained a bright golden tone which had defied any inclination to grow darker with age. His skin was clear and fair; his sparkling blue eyes depicted a sure beauty, though with a natural mischievious gleam behind them — a mischief which was more than just suggested, he was widely known to live it, for he was a man with a bit of an ill reputation. Though he was wealthy and noble, and when one really examined his character and put all his virtues and vices into consideration he was clearly not a *bad man*; it was nevertheless undeniable that he was possessed of some very bad habits and wicked ways.

His most consistent wickedness was a fondness for women. Married women, in particular. Married, but not to him. Why this preference? Well, for one, when they were married already to someone else, they had little personal interest toward marrying him, and he found that took a weight off the interaction. Secondly, the married women were occasioned a bit more freedom around him than the single girls. A young maiden, he could see little more of than for a few minutes worth of dancing at a crowded party; a married women might invite him to her own home, knowing her husband was away or occupied, and enjoy a nice private evening with him — not necessarily even with intent to enjoy any activities that could not have been done in public, but merely to have the relief that at last they did not *need* to be public. It could be a night of no more than sitting together reading books, but it could be done *tête-à-tête* rather than in the presence of four chaperones and all the lady's family members. For his looks, wealth and status he was considered a very desirable match, and many unmarried girls went away in disappointment for having failed to attract his attention; but the fact was if he had to spend his time among women, he preferred the married ones.

Of course this had led to a few quarrels with husbands. He had never yet fought a duel to the death, but he currently held a 50-50 on whether he was winner or loser in a few first-blood matches. A long raised scar from his shoulder to his sternum was the result of such a battle, the only one he had fought with swords; a dark, round scar from a bullet through the arm was another memento.

And here he was today, at dawn atop Solsbury Hill, to find out whether he should gain another loss or another win for his record.

The rival husband, Sir Joshua Hartley, wore an expression that indicated he might not care that the fight was only supposed to be first-blood, in which the loser would be only the man who first received an injury, no matter how minor. Legally, to kill an opponent in a duel was considered murder; though it was very well known and understood that the courts tended to sympathize with a man who had done such in defense of his honor.

The seconds finished loading the silvery pistols, and each handed one to his respective friend. Pink tinted sunlight shone at them through the smog of the city below, making the white glints of light off the guns almost painfully bright.

Sir Joshua's second, a middle-aged man who looked to be a servant, started trying to convince the men to abandon the duel. "Come now, it will not make a difference anymore — the business is done with — you needn't risk your life on account of that whore —"

Sir Joshua, hearing his wife referred to as "that whore" seemed to just aggravate all the more. He gnashed his teeth, secure in his determination to shoot *someone*.

Winthrope himself would have been happy to cancel this duel — he had no personal honor to defend in this matter, and it was not as if he intended to marry that woman even if her husband got blasted to death on her account. When this whole mess had started he had given serious consideration to just calling for the magistrate and having this lunatic Sir Joshua taken away for threatening him, but unfortunately, he had been pulled into too many duels in his life already for anyone to take him seriously were he to suddenly say he had no interest in fighting more.

Sir Joshua had chosen a short-range gunfight, suggesting he was probably a pretty bad shot himself. They were going to be firing from a mere three paces.

The duellists were herded to back to back position by the seconds. A quick rundown of the rules were recited for their benefit: no turning and running, no bending down or trying to shield the body, if the gun went off by mistake it still counted as a shot, and any injury which proved to bleed would be a sufficient call for the end of the fight.

Sir Joshua's man began the count: one, two, three. The fighters took their steps, and now stood a short distance apart from one another.

"And now turn..." was the instruction. "Aim your weapons... and... fire."

Lionel fired — and missed!

From the other side there was a click. Then again a click. But no shot. Sir Joshua's gun had jammed. He was frantically meddling with his pistol, trying to unstick the trigger. He shook it. He pulled it. Then suddenly, it went off — discharging a bullet right into his own foot. Sir Joshua screamed and fell as blood began gushing out of his shoe.

Happy enough with that outcome, Lionel tossed his pistol into the dirt, collected his second, and headed immediately back for his house in the town, thinking that after such an eventful morning, a breakfast of a half dozen Bath buns and some brandy punch was going to be required.

"Everything will be lovely and fun," Fanny assured her mistress, who was very much fretting about their situation in the town. The two women had reached Bath on the previous evening and taken rooms at the very first inn they could find, after an exhausting six days of travel. Agnes was up and already anxious to ready things for her husband's certain arrival in a few days. This inn they were at might not do for him — it was good quality but it was noisy and far from the center of town. He would probably prefer another place. It was early August, so the season in Bath was only just beginning. It might be possible to find a better situation if she were to hurry.

After a light breakfast of punch and bread, Agnes went out at once with Fanny so that the Rowereighs might find a nicer place to reside for their stay, than the noisy old inn. This hunt was actually something of an adventure for Agnes, as a task of this much importance had never been left completely to her before — she had always had some help, from either her parents at home, or from a steward or housekeeper at Rowereigh Castle. She took the endeavor seriously, and after walking about the town for several hours, she came upon a very nice hotel, new and fashionable in its construction, attached to a pretty public garden, and not a far walk from the famous Pump Room. This, she decided, would be her new seat while staying in Bath. She nervously made arrangements with the hoteliers, who found it unusual for a lady to be traveling alone but who nonetheless were made confident that she was a woman with money and was whom she said she was. After taking the names of her accountants she was shown to the best suite of rooms available. Fanny was sent back to the old inn along with a porter to help collect their baggage and transfer it to the new place.

Agnes was left on her own and was looking rather bored with all her personal items still at large, so the concierge suggested she might like to pass some time by walking through the gardens around the hotel, a pleasure for which subscriptions were normally sold by the fortnight. However, as a guest at the hotel, he arranged to allow her a free examination of the grounds to test whether she might enjoy it or not. It was a lovely garden indeed, done in a very naturalistic style and including Chinese-style bridges, rope swings and even a maze; and to her surprise, she discovered that around the side of the building was a public breakfast taking place. This event was evidently a daily custom of the hotel and gardens. The people that were gathered looked to be a mixed crowd of both wealthy and middling sorts.

Struck that perhaps this moment might be a good time for taking some refreshment after her long walk, she meandered over, took an empty seat at a bench, and at once was asked by the waiter if she was to be followed by the rest of her party? She acknowledged that no, she was alone — though realizing she was at risk of being mistaken for a prostitute or other disreputable woman, she was sure to mention also that she was a guest at the hotel and her servants were detained elsewhere. For a moment she considered going back inside and forgetting all about the breakfast, but decided that needless shame should not prevent her from feeding if she was hungry, and particularly when she had perfectly valid reasons for coming solo. She ordered herself some coffee and cold rolls, and patiently waited for them all by herself. She had not received the food before she was approached by a man and woman of the *ton* who had been eating a few benches over.

"I do beg pardon," said the lady, "if I disturb you, or if I have made a mistake in approaching, but you resemble somebody I have been acquainted with. Are you not Agnes Summersby, the daughter of Sir William Summersby?"

Agnes looked up and, after a moment, recognized the face of this woman to be an old friend from her short-lived school days: Susannah Alnwick had been her name then. The eyes and nose and carnelian-red hair were much as ever, though nearly ten years had passed since they'd known one another. Susannah was now grown up into a fine woman, plump but nowhere near fat, and perhaps lacking a little in physical beauty but with such a genuine joyfulness about her that any failure of looks was easy to ignore. Apparently, Agnes had not changed much since school herself, if she was so instantly to be recognized. Agnes confirmed her identity and that she was now the wife of Howard Rowereigh, Baronet. Of course this required explaining her husband's absence, and that he intended to join with her in a few days, but that she was alone in town for the time being. Susannah revealed that she too was married, readily introduced Agnes to her very agreeable spouse Mr. Gregory DeWitte, and invited her old friend to come sit at their breakfast bench rather than be left to eat all alone. Agnes agreed and had her order moved to the new location. It seemed that the DeWittes were breakfasting with several other fashionable friends that afternoon; sitting at the table were some other men and women, ages ranging from twenties to fifties, all dressed up to be seen. Agnes was suddenly become aware of her comparatively simple garments; she had dressed for a walk, not for dining.

A smiling older lady, wearing expensive but tasteful silk clothing, asked Mrs. DeWitte, "Will you introduce us to your friend?"

The door was opened: this meant introductions could be made all around (though Mrs. DeWitte had anticipated as much, for she had not been so presumptuous as to ask Agnes to the table without first consulting the others.) Everyone rose for their new arrival. Susannah DeWitte introduced Agnes to the pleasant Lady Carvington, who had made the request; also at the table were Sir Harvey Townsted, Mr. and Mrs. Jameson, Mr. Meyer, Mr. and Mrs. Woodbead, and last but not least, for he was sitting at the farthest end of the table, Lord Winthrope, the highest ranking member of their array. In fact the group were the members of the Bath Poetry Society, who met for this breakfast each month to exchange news of fresh books in publication, or poets in need of sponsors. And of course, they talked of more common topics whenever the news in literature was insufficient. Agnes joined the group, and the breakfast conversation continued from whence it stood before her arrival. Mrs. DeWitte quickly filled in the blanks of her knowledge by whispering that Lord Winthrope had been in a duel that very morning.

"Not much of a battle, in truth," said Lord Winthrope. "My opponent did little more than shoot himself in his own foot." A giggle erupted about the table as the breakfasters envisioned the comical scene.

"If I may be permitted to inquire," said Agnes, "what was the duel concerning?"

"The usual problems," answered Lord Winthrope, as if he needed to say no more; and indeed there was a chuckle from the rest of the table, as if the meaning had been fully understood. Agnes determined that it would be impolite to ask for further explanation.

Sir Harvey then interjected a story of some occasion when he had been called upon to duel, but was saved from battle at the last moment by the seconds coming to some amiable arrangement. Lady Carvington added in a tale of how her brother had once served as a second in somebody's duel over a business arrangement gone sour. Agnes attended it all with a sort of cheerful disinterest. Soon the talk turned to the plot of some recent stageplay which involved a duel, and a few members of the party began speculating whether or not they might go to see it while it was running at the theatre.

Within the hour the decent period for having a breakfast was over, and the gardens began to close up. Guests from the party bid their farewells and hurried off to their own business. Since Agnes was staying at the hotel itself, she didn't have far to go; but she did make an invitation to her old friend Susannah to come see her at her rooms, especially if it could be done before the arrival of her husband — "for he is not well, and that is how we have come to stay in Bath."

Susannah DeWitte could tell from just the few mentions made of Sir Howard that the marriage, prestigious enough as it was, was not turning out happily for poor Agnes. The only reason for a bride of five months to speak with such a dismal desperation regarding her husband was if she were clinging to a final hope of turning things around. And now here she was traveling alone, which was virtually never done by a woman of Agnes's position — that much in and of itself could be taken to signify a problem. Poor girl. Susannah did not disclose these thoughts but promised to call upon Agnes the following day, and in the meantime began to privately scheme for a way to improve her friend's condition.

CHAPTER 4

Agnes immediately wrote to her husband word of where she was to be found, and had the letter posted to their home at Rowereigh Castle. She was not certain whether he might already have taken steps to join her or not, but she imagined with hope that he might be getting ready to leave just as her letter would arrive, in a few days. In case he would be already *en route*, though, she made certain to leave word at the local high points and inns as to her husband's identity and where he was to find her, should he turn up looking.

Afterward she went to oversee how Fanny and the porter, with the help of her coachman Mr. Randal who was finding quite too little to do with himself, were all getting on in unpacking the luggage. No problems there. And now, with all her duties taken care of, she could get on with her real purpose in town — to take the healing spa waters and recover her health. The inn at Harrogate had been set up with a link directly to the spa waters, but in Bath it seemed it was more common for the newer, nicer lodgings to require a bit of a trip to go to take the waters. It was certainly no far walk; she made it in 10 minutes. She did not even think it necessary to bring Fanny along to accompany. Her destination was The Pump Room.

Upon her entry, she was once again embarrassed to see that she was underdressed for what was actually taking place in her destination. Harrogate had been a little town where all the visitors were really there for the spas; Bath was a great city where people went to be seen, and the spa water was viewed as sort of a bonus. The Pump Room was bursting with fashionable folk, wearing top style, promenading and showing off. A drink or two of spa water was simply there to make them feel like they were doing something healthy and useful for themselves. The men were in cocked hats and breeches with stockings; the women were wearing silks and velvets trimmed in gold and embroidery. They were practically dressed for a ball. Musicians were playing tunes in a little nook overhead, giving a cheerful air to the room.

Agnes had brought a couple of nice outfits to Bath with her, including the silver satin gown she had used for a wedding dress; but the manner in which her life had fallen meant she had not had much time to invest in luxuries such as sewing or shopping for new clothing since the time of her becoming a wife; and the financial situation of her parents before that time meant she had always been accustomed to a frugal wardrobe. With this being the second time in a day she had been embarrassed by the state of her clothing, she made a mental note to do some shopping while she was in town. As it was, she endured more glances for coming in all alone than she did for being underdressed, but she didn't think too much about them. Whatever anyone else was there for, *she* had come for the waters. She went straight for the pump, and waited her turn to receive some of the special liquid from a servant woman who was distributing cupfuls. Agnes at last got her portion of water, tipped the servant, and drank deeply of the liquid. It was much milder, indeed, than the Harrogate water; surely it would agree well with Sir Howard's sensitive stomach.

Wanting to let the first glass of water settle before taking another, she decided to observe the promenade about the room and took in the sights of the fashionable men and women enjoying their leisurely afternoons; the silk gowns and cloth shoes, the lace trims and gold buttons, the fragrance of every imaginable cologne and perfume in which the *promenadeurs* had doused themselves.

At length Agnes took her second draught of Bath water, consumed it, and returned back to her own hotel. She inquired with the concierge about where the best dressmakers and shops were in the city, and took the notes up with her to her rooms. She spent the rest of the evening looking over her old wardrobe and determining whether or not she owned anything that shouldn't be either given away to the poor, or burnt. The chambermaid Fanny gained three second-hand gowns in consequence of this exercise.

The next morning, before breakfast, Agnes put on her second-best gown and had Mr. Randal drive her directly to the best dressmaker in Bath. Afterall, what point was there in having married Sir Howard if not to buy nice things? She ordered six new gowns from the dressmaker, made in the fashionable new Gothic mode, which the *couturer* expected to have ready for her in approximately six weeks.

Agnes then returned to the hotel, and ate a private breakfast — which she barely had time to finish before there was a knock at the door. Fanny answered, and found it was the hotel porter, who was announcing a visit from Mrs. DeWitte. The news was relayed, and Agnes asked that Mrs. DeWitte be sent up.

Once the two old friends were seated together, and the customary greetings dispensed with, they began to inquire after what had happened in each others' lives since their girlhood, and were able to be much more familiar with one another than the prior days' crowd had allowed for. Susannah told all about her happy and uneventful courtship with Mr. DeWitte, whose grandfather had been an Earl but whose father was a title-lacking younger son; but he owned some valuable livings and the two of them were now wedded and in perfect contentment. Agnes congratulated her friend on her good fortune and wished all the best for her. When it was Agnes's turn to talk, she told of her pleasant courtship and all the high hopes she had for her marriage to Sir Howard, the lovely wedding, but that "he had been rather poorly since that time."

"It is my recollection," pried Susannah, "that you yesterday did indicate he will be following you here to Bath?"

"Yes, when he is well enough for the trip. I believe, truly, he is in greater need of the water-cure than I. My illness was largely gone away after Harrogate."

"My poor friend, have you also been ill?" asked Susannah.

"Unhappily I had been growing so; but since taking the waters I have been much better."

"So that is why you have come here all alone!"

"Yes — and my hopes are very high, as I have only been here one day, and taken but two draughts of the water, and I am already feeling so much better than I have at any time since the wedding!"

Susannah had some suspicions, and tried to word the next question carefully so as not to influence the reply. "I would assume that you have not been much apart from Sir Howard since the marriage date?"

"I have not left his side until a week ago, when I set out on the journey."

What Susannah next wished to say was *How curious that you should so improve only once you've left his side,* but she held her tongue on that. Still, she could decipher that poor, optimistic Agnes had not been happy for so much as a day with her husband, and was now praying for a miracle cure from the spa to fix the trouble. Susannah herself was wed happily, but the same could not be said of her own parents; and she recognized the same aura of despair and desperation which was always born about her mother, now encircling poor Agnes. She had witnessed too many miseries in her parents to ever want to see someone else enduring such a life, and a passionate determination was formed in her breast to give Agnes whatever assistance was in her power, to relieve her of an unhappy situation.

"Well," said Susannah, "I could not be sure as to the custom in the midlands, but here in Bath it is extremely unusual for a lady to be going about town all by herself, with no companions either male or female. It is certainly never done by young ladies of our status. I should not allow my friend to make such a needless spectacle of herself! So, my dear Agnes, I beg of you, if you wish to go anyplace in town, call upon me; or if I am not available, send word to my good friend Lord Winthrope, whom you met at breakfast yesterday. I have spoken to him already and he has confirmed that he will be glad to accompany you."

"Lord Winthrope? Oh, I do appreciate the concern, Susannah, but do you really think a gentleman such as Lord Winthrope, whom I scarcely know, would be good company?"

"There is nothing improper in seeing him publicly; it is not as if he would be courting you. And it will certainly appear less strange if you are going about with *somebody*, than if you are with no one at all. That he risks his life in duelling for the sake of his honor should be testament to the goodness of his character."

"Alright, then. If you assert that he is man of good character, I will consider requesting his company — that is, only if you would be too inconvenienced, at some time, to join me yourself."

"If you would prefer it, I could arrange for Winthrope to join the two of us someplace, so that you might get to know him better yourself and feel easy at the thought of his company."

"If you think it might be for the best."

And thus did Susannah suggest that, on Monday, they might all take a trip to Westbury to see the white horse on the hillside; they would need to set out early in the day, as it was a ride of about five hours, but if they spent no more than an hour or two — and really, how long could one spend looking at a depiction of a horse? — they should be able to return to Bath by nightfall. Agnes expressed some concern that to be gone all day might deprive her of the necessary spa water she had come out for, but Susannah suggested that some might be collected in a bottle and taken along. At last, Agnes was convinced, and agreed to the plan.

CHAPTER 5

A glass oil-lamp went flying across the room, landed against a wall, and smashed to pieces, spraying shards and oil all across the crisp white wall-paint and the thick Turkish rug below. Its thrower, Lady Mary Hartley, was in the doorway, and was dismayed that she had missed her target: the face of Viscount Lionel Winthrope.

"Do you realize my husband is required to have his foot amputated because of what you have done?!" she shrieked in a rage.

Winthrope maintained a stern expression with furrowed brows, arms crossed aggressively over his chest. "A man who shoots so poorly that he cannot avoid hitting his own foot oughtn't be challenging anybody to a duel in the first place, no matter his reasons."

"How can you imagine yourself so blameless? You should have known what would happen! You shouldn't have been spending so much time with me!"

"You are quite correct. I will fix that immediately. Goodbye! The servants will show you out."

Lady Hartley could think of nothing else to do but oblige, and to storm off.

Outside of the house, Lady Hartley made her exit and crawled back into her own coach just in time to be observed by Mrs. Susannah DeWitte as she stepped out of hers. For women to call upon men was normally frowned upon, but it was so common an event at Lord Winthrope's house that most everyone had stopped caring some time ago about the female presence in his life. Bath was a town more forgiving than most, anyway.

Inside the townhouse, Susannah met with Lord Winthrope, who invited her to have tea in the dining room as the parlour was being cleaned up. Whilst they sipped at their tiny cups, Mrs. DeWitte explained that, as they had already discussed in a previous conversation, she had gone forward with inviting Lady Rowereigh to call upon him in order to spare her anymore embarrassing solo expeditions while awaiting her husband's arrival in town; and then produced the news and invitation for the trip to Westbury on Monday.

"It is five hours each way, so you and Agnes — that is, Lady Rowereigh — shall have plenty of time to become *acquainted*," Mrs. DeWitte assured with a suggestive tone.

"Ten hours in a coach with her?" he replied boredly. "Do you quite suppose she will prove so interesting?"

"I would not strive to introduce the two of you in such a way, unless I felt confident the two of you could benefit from one another's company. Besides, Mr. DeWitte and I will be with you... part of the way, at least."

"I tell you, I am not at all desirous of feigning so much as a flirtation with a woman whom I might find less than appealing; and that is for her own sake as well as mine. I hope it is understood that I make no guarantees about what I will or will not do with the lady: you are asking me to meet her, and I will oblige you as far as that."

"You know I am no procuress — I am not seeking to force you into anything — I simply think the two of you will get on very well together. This poor girl needs a few happy days in her life, before her husband returns to her side; a gentleman like you, who has stories and knows something of the world, might be just the person to cheer her up with his attentions. I am perfectly aware that your behavior with married women is not so indecent as the gossip-mongers would claim; you have, for instance, always been a perfect gentleman with me. Like a brother."

"I thank for you the favorable compliment. In that case, shall I bring some *Ossian* to entertain us in the coach?"

"I should prefer something without a proven tendency to inspire suicide."

The following Monday, with a copy of *The Satires of Juvenal* on his lap, Winthrope rode with

Mr. and Mrs. DeWitte to collect Agnes from her hotel.

They called on the porter to announce them; of course he did announce them, and they were invited by the lady to wait inside. Almost as soon as they entered her suite, she emerged in her second-best dress (a white and rose colored walking gown straight off a fashion plate of a few years ago), carrying a heavy basket full of corked bottles of spa-water. The gentlemen hurried to help her with it.

The group went together into the coach and set out at once. The inside of the box smelled deliciously of the food packed into picnic baskets, which the DeWittes had prepared for later consumption.

As the coach bounced its way out of Bath, the group became more intimately acquainted. Mr. DeWitte was a nice, good, nice man. One couldn't say anything against him, yet he seemed to have nothing else about him except that he was nice and good. He was interested in whatever interested you, because he was so nice. He always had some nice, neutral comment to add to the conversation. He was nicely dressed and had nice features. He was very nicely matched with his much more aggressive and cunning wife, who seemed to have been put on Earth by God Himself to make sure that this good, nice man should not be bored to death.

Of course Lord Winthrope was a more complicated creature. He lived in the world, knew he had to make certain accommodations to the needs and ways of the world, but despised the artificiality of the world; and he was rich enough that he could get away with some degree of despising these things, just as long as he was reserved in imposing it on others. So he was polite; he dressed to fashion; he only talked about his political views at Parliament; he smiled at children and held doors open for women and helped old ladies across the street. But he would also befriend whoever he wanted, even if that person's company were socially forbidden for some reason; and might reject friendship, even if it were deemed appropriate or advantageous, if he didn't truly like the person's company. If he merely feigned a fondness for them, they'd usually find out the truth eventually, and hate him just as much for it as they would if he had been upfront about disliking them. So what was the point? His viewpoints earned him more enemies than friends, but the friends he had tended to be very close and very loyal.

And as to Agnes, she was reserved, but of course cordial toward the men who were sharing the coach. This was actually the first *outing* for pleasure she had had in over six months, and secretly her heart was pounding with joy at having the chance to finally do something fun, that had nothing to do with medicine.

To break the ice, it was suggested that Lord Winthrope read from the copy of Juvenal he had brought along, and so he began:

And must I, while hoarse Codrus perseveres

To force his Theseid on my tortured ears,

Hear, always hear, nor once the debt repay?

Must this, unpunish'd, pour his comic lay?

I too can write — and, at a pedant's frown,

Once pour'd my fustian rhetoric on the town,

And idly proved that Sylla, far from power,

Had pass'd, unknown to fear, the tranquil hour:—

Now I resume my pen; for since we meet

Such swarms of desperate bards in every street,

'Twere vicious clemency to spare the oil,

And hapless paper, they are sure to spoil.

But why I choose, adventurous, to retrace

The Auruncan's route, and in the arduous race

Follow his burning wheels, attentive hear,

If leisure serve, and truth be worth your ear.

When the soft eunuch weds; and the bold fair

Tilts at the Tuscan boar, with bosom bare;

When one that oft, since manhood first appear'd,

Hath trimm'd the exuberance of this sounding beard,

In wealth outvies the senate; when a vile

And low-bred reptile, from the slime of Nile,

Crispinus, while he gathers now, now flings
His purple open, fans his summer rings;
And, as his fingers sweat beneath the freight,
Cries, "Save me from a gem of greater weight!"
'Tis hard the rage of satire to restrain:—
For who so slow of heart, so dull of brain,
So patient of the town, as to forbear;
When Matho passes, in a new-built chair
Stuff'd with himself, follow'd, in equal state,
By that false friend, who to the imperial hate
Betray'd one noble, and now seeks to wrest
The poor remains of greatness from the rest:
Whom Massa dreads, Latinus, trembling, plies
With a fair wife, and anxious Carus buys!
When those supplant thee in thy dearest rights,
Who earn rich legacies by active nights,
Those whom, the surest, shortest way to rise,
The widow's itch, advances to the skies!
Not that an equal rank her minions hold:—
Just to their various powers, she metes her gold,
And Proculeius mourns his scanty share,
While Gillo triumphs, hers and nature's heir!

Ye Powers! — What rage, what frenzy fires my brain,
When that false guardian, with his crowded train,
Chokes up the street, and leaves his orphan charge
To prostitution, and the world at large!
While great Pelides sought superior bliss,
And toy'd and wanton'd with his master-miss.
Who would not, reckless of the swarm he meets,
Fill his wide tablets in the public streets
With angry verse? When, through the midday glare,
Borne by six slaves, and in an open chair,
The forger comes, who owes his lavish state
To a wet seal and a fictitious date;
Comes, like the soft Maecenas, lolling by,
And impudently braves the public eye!
Or the rich dame, who stanch'd her husband's thirst
With generous bowls, but drugg'd them deeply first!
O! who can see the stepfather impure,
The greedy daughter to his bed allure;
See, and suppress his feelings while he sees,
Unnatural brides, and stripling debauchees?
When crimes like these on every side arise,
Anger shall give what mother-wit denies,

And pour, in Nature and the Nine's despite,
Such strains as I, or Cluvienus, write!
Whatever wild desires have swell'd the breast,
Whatever passions have the soul possess'd;
Joy, Sorrow, Fear, Love, Hatred, Transport, Rage,
Shall form the motley subject of my page.
And when could Satire boast so fair a field?
Say, when did Vice a richer harvest yield?
When did fell Avarice so inflame the mind?
And when the lust of play so curse mankind?
But when Lucilius, fired with virtuous rage,
Waves his keen falchion o'er a guilty age,
The conscious villain shudders at his sin,
And burning blushes speak the pangs within;
Cold drops of sweat from every member roll,
And growing terrors harrow up his soul!
Then tears of shame, and dire revenge succeed —
Say; have you ponder'd well the adventurous deed?
Now — ere the trumpet sounds — your strength debate;
The soldier once engaged repents too late.
Yet I must write: and since these iron times
From living knaves preclude my angry rhymes,

I point my pen against the guilty dead,
And pour its gall on each obnoxious head.

Agnes listened to the poem; Lord Winthrope read it well. She considered the ancient author's accusations and thought on how so many of his complaints seemed valid even yet. Of course Mr. DeWitte said something nice about the reading, and Mrs. DeWitte spoke favorably of it while simultaneously trying to discern the reaction of her protegé. When she asked what Agnes thought, Agnes replied by wondering if the passage about the "Bold Fair" fighting Tuscan boars was real or an exaggeration.

"Oh yes," said Lord Winthrope, "it is true. There is even a footnote to the text... 'Under Domitian such instances were common; for he not only exhibited combats of men with wild beasts, but of women also; and the noblest of both sexes were sometimes engaged in them!'"

"Well," said Mrs. DeWitte with a laugh, "if a Tuscan boar came charging at me, I should drop whatever I was about and run!"

And such idle and interesting conversation continued, and more Juvenal was read whenever there was a lull, until after many hours they reached the white horse on the hill at Westbury. It was much as the name suggests: an image of a horse, made of white chalk, colored upon the side of a hill. The party stopped their coach at a suitable viewing spot, and sat down for their picnic luncheon. Agnes and Lionel began talking to one another with increasing interest: she learned he was a Viscount, unmarried, owned some properties in both Britain and abroad, had done the Grand Tour before Napoleon shut it down, had taken credit for writing some operas as a favor to a friend who couldn't get them performed under his own name, owned the distillery that made her favorite brandy, spoke five languages (two of them dead), and had once acted as a spy in France.

She, in turn, told him only that she was married, and refused to say anything more on the topic — this was not out of shyness or unfriendliness, but out of embarrassment, and the horrifying realization that talking of her husband or of her own accomplishments would only sour the fun mood that had been established.

CHAPTER 6

The foursome enjoyed their meal of cheese, bread, cold ham and candied walnuts with cider and plenty of spa water to drink. After eating the food and tossing the trash into the bushes, they decided to take the hike up the hillside to gain a closer inspection of the white horse. It required the party to cut across a field, through a little grove of trees, then up the hill. Mr. DeWitte took Mrs. DeWitte by the arm and Lord Winthrope took the arm of Agnes, to guide them along. The duos smiled their way across the warm grass and into the shady leaves of the grove. In there, the DeWitte's deliberately tried to keep a bit of distance from the other couple — just in case their presence might be found intrusive.

Lionel was aware of what the DeWitte's wished from him, and had admitted when the idea was first proposed that he didn't much like the notion of being under pressure to favor the woman or not, and he had refused absolutely to feign any affection for her if it should not have naturally come. Fortunately, he was discovering her to be, in fact, very agreeable to him.

Agnes, meanwhile, was on cloud nine. This was the life she had been picturing for herself when she had agreed to marriage — fond days of friends and companionship, fun and a sense of importance, with a bright future that promised many happy returns. Completely absorbed in the moment, she clung to Lord Winthrope's hand as he led her through the greenage.

At length they emerged at the foot of the destination hillside and gradually worked their way up. Breathless and pink-faced they reached, at last, the horse. Little blue butterflies were perched all over its white surface, basking in the late-summer's warmth. The presence of the humans disturbed a few of the number, which fluttered skyward and into the visitors' faces.

Lionel and Agnes sat down in a sunny patch to rest after the climb. Mrs. DeWitte seemed as if she would do likewise, but made an excuse that the grass was too wet and she would need to find a different spot some distance away. Mr. DeWitte followed his wife.

More or less alone together, Lionel and Agnes were seated with only a small distance separating one from the other. Their hearts were still beating in a unified rhythm from the climb. Or was it from the climb? They talked gaily of unimportant subjects, then of increasingly important topics. They found they had attitudes and mindsets which complimented one another, and certainly on paper would have seemed a good match. There was more than paper going on here though, and soon, Agnes was finding herself longing to cry out, *If only I were not married!* When Mrs. DeWitte finally reapproached, asking if they wished to return to the coach, Lionel and Agnes were still as breathless and blushing as when they first had sat down together.

The two couples quickly journeyed back down the hillside, and made the trek back to the coach. They gathered up their belongings and packed back into the cabin, intending to make the return journey to Bath. But after about 40 minutes Mrs. DeWitte began to complain of feeling unwell. Lionel rolled his eyes at the charade, but said nothing. Mrs. DeWitte began complaining that the shaking of the coach was too much for her, and she that it was necessary for her to stop and rest somewhere. She had her husband call out to the coachman to stop at the next inn they might see. In a fortuitously short time they found a rustic little inn, within a nothing of a village called Heywood, where Mrs. DeWitte declared she would stop. Agnes wanted to get out with her, but her friend was insistent: "No, no — hurry back to Bath, or else you and Lord Winthrope will be forced to stay the night here. I am too unwell, I cannot make the trip today, something I ate must have disordered my stomach too much for a journey. Mr. DeWitte must stay to attend me. Willy — " she said, addressing the coachman, "take our guests back home to Bath, and you shall return to this same inn tomorrow morning for Mr. DeWitte and I. I am in no condition to travel further today."

The DeWittes bade a quick farewell to their friends and urged them be on their way to reach Bath by nightfall.

As the clop clop clop of the horse's hooves started gaining its rhythm afresh, Lord Winthrope asked if Agnes would have anymore interest in hearing some Juvenal. Agnes found that the concern for her friend was fast transforming into an embarrassing discomfort at being left alone in a coach with Lord Winthrope for the remainder of their long trip back to Bath. She swiftly agreed to the poetry, but as he read, her mind was unfocused upon the ancient author's words. She had always imagined herself to be perfect wife material, taken pride in her perfect fidelity and attention to her husband, and now here she was in this rather questionable situation... and to make it worse, it was not as if she genuinely had no interest in this man before her. Without a doubt, she herself would have looked down upon any woman described to be in a position such as this! But of course *she* would behave herself. She was not an animal or some "bold fair" without a sense of propriety. She was a happily married woman — well, maybe not happily, but she was *properly* married, in any event. Her poor, sick husband was perhaps on his way to join her in Bath this very moment. Her duty was to him. Lord Winthrope was simply a pleasant friend, and there was no reason to bar that — was that not why Susannah had recommended him?

Lord Winthrope was at this time finishing the poem:

> "...*And every prudent chief must sure desire*
> *That still the worthiest should the most acquire;*
> *That those who merit, their rewards should have:*
> *Trappings, and chains, and all that decks the brave!*"

The pause after these words indicated the end of the reading. Agnes smiled as pleasantly as she could. "What lovely recitation, Lord

Winthrope. You must permit me to hear some more."

"I am afraid, madam, there is no more to be heard; that poem was the last in the book. Unless you should like me to go back and read some of them afresh?"

"Oh. No, thank you; that will do."

Lord Winthrope looked at Agnes's face and wondered if he had done something wrong; her cheerful spirit seemed to have faded and she was growing quiet and somber. Whereas before she had been a bright, open book, she was now like something locked up in a chest and hidden in the back of a closet under a stack of clothes that no longer fit, and unless he could lose 10 pounds at once he might never see it again. He decided to inquire: "Lady Rowereigh, are you quite alright?"

"Hm? Naturally. Why should you ask?"

"You seem to have gone rather quiet, if I may observe."

"Oh..." Agnes thought of a quick excuse. "I am simply worried for Mrs. DeWitte. I hope it was not irresponsible of us to leave her."

He smiled a little. "I am sure it is nothing but a sudden onset of hypochondria."

"Hypochondria? I'm sorry, what is that?"

"It means that her illness is entirely imaginary. I should be straightforward with you: she has deliberately — and entirely for her own reasons — decided that we should have the coach to ourselves for the journey back to Bath."

Agnes was perplexed at that. "Well, why should she imagine *that* a fitting thing to do?"

"I only know what she is about; I know not the why of it," he fibbed, confident that speculating about Agnes's marriage to Sir Howard was not the proper thing to do right now. "But she has requested I should do my utmost to keep you entertained and amused on this journey. We are out of Juvenal. What else would you have?"

"Oh. I am at a loss... do you know any other poems?"

Winthrope paused for a moment trying to think if there were a poem he knew in entirety by rote. Poetry was another vice of his, and he had a goodly collection of it at his home. After a moment's contemplation he began:

"Sound the flute!
Now it's mute.
Birds delight
Day and night;
Nightingale
In the dale,
Lark in sky,
Merrily,
Merrily, merrily, to welcome in the year.
Little boy,
Full of joy;
Little girl,
Sweet and small;
Cock does crow,
So do you;
Merry voice,

Infant noise,
Merrily, merrily, to welcome in the year.
Little lamb,
Here I am;
Come and lick
My white neck;
Let me pull
Your soft wool;
Let me kiss
Your soft face;
Merrily, merrily, we welcome in the year."

Admittedly, he felt a little foolish as he continued reciting; though the poem was composed as an innocent story of children frolicking in a pasture, the references to kissing and licking started to seem a little out of turn in the tense situation at hand. It was all born of some kind of deep-hidden mental word-game anyway: he was unconsciously associating the lamb with its Latin term *agnus* and that with the name of Agnes.

Happily, Agnes knew no Latin, and was more worried about whether her own thoughts were too perverted, than she was about his. Still, Lionel could see she was remaining ill at ease. He considered what he had to do, decided his course, and then rose and banged his fist on the door to get the driver's attention.

"Driver — stop the coach!"

The driver reigned in the horses and brought the coach to a halt. Lionel looked at Agnes. "I can sense that Mrs. DeWitte's ideas might not have been altogether appropriate for our circumstances. I am going to leave you here, that you may finish the journey in privacy; you may keep the copy of Juvenal for your entertainment." He began opening the door.

Agnes was surprised. "Wait! You mean to abandon yourself out here?"

"Better here than 10 minutes hence," he said, stepping away from the cabin. "The inn, where Mr. and Mrs. DeWitte stay, is only an half-hour's walk behind us; and if I wait with them, I can ride in the coach when it returns tomorrow. I bid you good-day, Lady Rowereigh; and wish you a pleasant journey."

He began to leave. Agnes was struck instantly with a sense of guilt and sorrow. She called out to him: "Lord Winthrope! Wait!" He stopped. She continued, "Please get back in the coach."

He hesitated. "Are you sure that is your wish?"

"Most sure. I wouldn't hear of anything else. I am sorry if my demeanor gave you any impression that your presence was unwanted..."

Of course, like a good gentleman, Lord Winthrope put all the blame on himself and assured Lady Rowereigh that she had done nothing whatsoever to offend him. After some further urging, he returned to the vehicle, and the coach resumed its progress toward Bath.

In the compartment, there remained a bit of an awkward silence; but much less heavy than before, for now both Lord Winthrope and Lady

Rowereigh were confident that she did truly desire his presence, and that it had not simply been forced upon her. She now made an effort to recreate a light and cheerful mood by inquiring after his family. He, in turn, related stories of his mother and sister; he was fond of both of them, and suggested that Lady Rowereigh should one day meet them. She approved of the idea, and lamented that she had not siblings of her own. Though she said nothing, she began to wonder whether his sister would get on well with her, or if they could be like sisters themselves; and privately, he wondered the same.

Soon the tension was abated and they were back to chatting mirthfully with one another. The time seemed to fly by, and when the coach began to undulate across the hills outside the city of Bath, there was disappointment in Agnes's eyes. Gazing out the window, she could see that the sun was just beginning to set and the city lights were taking over.

"I do not think I shall have a happy day like this again for a long time," she confessed, wistfully. "I do wish it were not to end so soon."

"Well..." Lord Winthrope began thoughtfully, then silenced himself as if he was thinking better of it. Agnes pried for more information. "It being Monday evening, there is an assembly each week on this night, at the New Rooms."

Agnes laughed. "Oh, we are not dressed for a ball! I think I have not a single gown suited to it, even. Besides, what should people think to see us there together?"

"They should probably take us for a young couple dancing. I certainly am not attached to anyone — and you, are attached to somebody that nobody has ever met."

Smiling, Agnes's eyes went wide as she imagined it: she could hurry to her hotel and change into her silver gown — she wouldn't be the prettiest woman there but she would look acceptable — and she could send her own coach round to get Lord Winthrope after he had changed... they would attend the ball and dance away the night hand in hand... but then reality settled back in, and she knew it was not just impossible; it was indecent. She was married, to Sir Howard Rowereigh, who was sick through no fault of his own (or, to her knowledge no fault) and who deserved her love and devotion. It was his money paying for this comfortable stay in Bath. She sweetly rejected the offer of Lord Winthrope, and to put him at ease began pretending to be anxious for returning to her own rooms to rest.

As the DeWitte's coach rolled up to the hotel, Agnes and Lionel began to bid each other fond farewells.

"I do hope," he said to her, "that if you found this day enjoyable, that you should not begrudge me an opportunity to escort you someplace again in the future."

"I would like that," she replied. "I do not know how soon before my husband arrives in town, but even then — there should surely be no objection to our acquaintanceship, should there? We have done nothing shameful or unbecoming."

"No, not at all. There should be no reason at all to complain," he agreed, though knowing a little better deep within his fiery, impassioned heart.

They bid their final farewells, and Agnes made her way into the hotel and up to her suite, where she immediately changed for bed, and laid down to dream sweet dreams about her new friend, Lord Lionel Winthrope.

And far away, in an altogether other part of the country, Sir Howard was dictating, through one of his servants, a letter to his wife in Bath, declaring that he had changed his mind and now had no plans to make the trip. The dictation was difficult because he had to continually pause his speech in order to regurgitate into a sticky, stinking bucket which he kept at his side. But he explained that he had not been a believer in the spa cure to begin with, and could not now justify the toll that such a long trip would surely take upon him and his health. However, he did provide his expressed permission to do whatever she felt was needed to regain her own health, and if that meant staying for a few weeks in Bath, he would not oppose her in any way. He had the letter sealed and prepared for posting first thing in the morning. Howard really did adore his wife, when he was not too doped up on opium — his courtship had been sincere, afterall — and he did fondly wish to have her back at home, healthy and happy as she had been when he had first married her. After taking a fresh dose of laudanum, he went to bed and dreamt surreal dreams of he with his gay and cheerful wife, in better days, which his addled brain did not know would never come.

CHAPTER 7

When Lionel woke in the morning, the very first thing on his mind was how Agnes was doing. He wondered if he ought to call upon her after breakfast. Surely she had be wanting to visit the Pump Room to take the waters — perhaps he might invite her? As he broke his own fast, his mind was nowhere near the food the servants laid out or the tastefully decorated home in which he dwelt: mentally he was all with Agnes, showing her about the town, introducing her to friends, even just being with her quietly...

And when Agnes woke from her slumber, her first thought was whether she might see Lord Winthrope today, whether she should invite him to the public breakfast at the hotel, whether she might be able to find a nice enough dress to attend the Thursday assembly with him...

Oh, Mrs. DeWitte's wild scheme had been correct! Lord Winthrope and Lady Rowereigh did benefit from knowing one another. The chemicals of love were flowing all through them and they were both already drunk and addicted thereon. The only means to having more, was for each to see the other again.

Lionel put on his morning outfit and imagined he might take a perfectly innocent and respectable walk to pass the time and get some exercise. Maybe he would try to catch a look at the vauxhall gardens, which were so lovely in appearance, and which were right by her hotel, and if he was in the area already, perhaps it would not be too improper to call upon her — Oh, who was he kidding? He would just call upon Lady Rowereigh directly.

Lionel's townhouse was only a short walk from Lady Rowereigh's hotel. He decided to take the longest possible route, and believed he had taken a lengthy and leisurely pace in making the walk, but was astounded when he checked his pocket-watch to learn that it had not even needed five minutes to complete. It was a little early for visiting unexpected — not yet noon. He decided that, on second thought, maybe he would take that walk in the gardens to pass a little bit of time.

How surprised he was to discover Lady Rowereigh there amongst the shrubs, wearing her bonnet and shaded by a parasol: she had decided to take a stroll into the garden herself to pass the time, because she had felt certain that it was still much too early in the day to send a message to Lord Winthrope asking him to call upon her.

Transfixed eyes upon each other, they spoke with perfect courtesy of how happy and surprised they were to run into one another so unexpectedly. Then, because Lady Rowereigh clearly had not been properly shown about the town, Lord Winthrope hooked her by the arm and offered to take her around.

He led her by the famous bath houses which were the city's namesake, and then showed her a large pit being dug out: he revealed that, during the construction of another building, an ancient Roman structure — like from the time of Juvenal — had been discovered underground, and it was now being excavated; and right nearby, some Saxon graves from the time of King Alfred were found, with stone coffins. Then to the Guildhall they went, where he showed her some of the artifacts and read her the Latin inscriptions on the stones and tablets that had been found. Some of them had been discovered right under the hotel where she was lodging. Agnes tried to picture living in the same places back in Roman times; but based on what Juvenal said she was inclined to think it had probably all been very similar to the life she knew now, apart from the topless women fighting boars.

They wasted a few hours in this way, glad for an excuse to spend time with one another. They decided to have a supper together at an inn, and as the sky grew pink they realized it was essential to depart one another's company, and Agnes was deposited back at her hotel.

When Lionel returned home, he sank down into a Chippendale chair and thought about his situation. This was not his usual behavior towards his married women; usually they were just like any of his other friends. Married women were not as silly as the single girls and were not as aggressive and competitive as men tended to be; that was all. Sometimes the women had made the mistake of falling in love with him — sometimes he even made the mistake of indulging those ones with more than mere friendly attention; but even when he did, it was understood to all be a silly, temporary thing to pass some time. Agnes was a different matter: his heart was beating for her. He wanted to be with her all the time. Why, if she *had* been single, he would be courting her right now, and probably would already be doing ridiculous things like contemplating what wedding rings to buy, or introducing her to his family members.

Then he remembered, he *had* promised to introduce her to his family. His sister, Lady Georgiana Murer, was right here in Bath for the season — his mother was a bit more of a distance away at the family estate in Yorkshire. Perhaps this week he could find an excuse to bring together Georgiana and Agnes. Certainly it would help Agnes to know more people in town than only himself and Mrs. DeWitte and the poetry club.

Thus it fell that on Wednesday, they went to the riverside together, and after walking around for over four hours and picking up a bit of sunburn, they paid a visit to the best confectioner in town and ate sweets till they were ready to explode.

Thursday, they went to the game rooms and played whist against a friendly married couple from Manchester until everyone was turned out to make room for the fancy ball that night.

Friday they went to the Pump Room, with taking of the waters being a mere perk of the visit; they were there for the promenade and to enjoy the music.

On Saturday they went to the tennis court and played together; never having played tennis before, Agnes was awful at it, but Lord Winthrope started letting her win — after a while.

Sunday, Lord Winthrope attended the Laura Chapel with Lady Rowereigh, instead of his usual Saint Michael's Church, and they tried to think of nice, pure, holy thoughts as they sat together.

Having now been seen together just about every day by everyone in town, their association with one another was widely known. Of course Lord Winthrope was a known person about the city; but the woman was a newcomer who hadn't even been signed into the Subscription Book. People began to wonder about her identity, though knowing Lord Winthrope's habits, it could be assumed she was another one of his married ladies... but then again, this woman was being seen with no other man. Could she be a *single* woman he was courting so fiercely? But if that were so, wasn't it strange that she never had a chaperone?

Mrs. DeWitte felt a mixture of pride and shame when her Monday evening dinner-party's conversation turned to the question of just who was the lady that Lord Winthrope was going about with. Now, it was a semi-official rule in the society of Bath that all repeaters of lies and scandal be shunned by all company (except such as have been guilty of the same crime) — but it was hardly a lie that Lord Winthrope was being seen constantly accompanied by a lone mystery woman. Wisely, Mrs. DeWitte put forward no absolutes and merely promised she would inquire with Lord Winthrope next time she might see him; and Mr. DeWitte put the company at ease by sincerely remarking how nice it was that Lord Winthrope had found a woman he seemed so happy with.

Meanwhile, at Winthrope's house, the mystery couple were sitting on a bench in the library, looking together over Winthrope's personal copy of Blake's *Songs of Innocence and Experience*. The colorful pages were tinted by the artist himself. They had read past *Spring*, the poem which Lord Winthrope had been embarrassed to recite on the way back from the white horse, and their love-sick minds were again reading all kind of hidden things into the poet's words, which seemed to apply perfectly to them. Surely, *The Angel* was some kind of omen from God that they should not let love pass by! *Little Boy Lost* was doubtless some occult spirit warning against premature marriage such as Agnes had done! *The Lamb* was certainly all about Agnes! What a fortuitous choice of book was this! The excess importance they were putting upon the trifling words of the poet was making the book into the most gripping and exciting of reads.

"O rose, thou art sick," read Lord Winthrope. "The invisible worm/That flies in the night in the howling storm/Has found out thy bed of crimson joy/And his dark, secret love does thy life destroy!"

"How sad for the rose!" said Agnes, reading herself as that rose and her husband as that invisible worm. "If only a rose had legs to escape from it!"

"That is why she is calling the gardener," joked Lionel, looking over the illustration of a rotting rosebush with a single bright blossom at the bottom of the page, which was being eaten by a worm whilst a symbolic screaming woman poked her head out from the petals. He was pointing at the woman. Agnes had to laugh at that.

"Oh, but let us be serious," she said. "My husband drains the life from me — I had no disorder of my health until I married him. He is a contagion, I think. But soon... soon he will be here in town," she said (for she had not yet received the man's letter stating otherwise.) "I dread that the happiness I have found here will be drained off again at once."

Lionel could make no denial, even to her, that he was not looking forward to the arrival of her husband. "Perhaps when he arrives, he can busy himself with the doctors and leave you to your own pursuits."

"He may be repulsive to me, but he *is* my husband, and I have a duty to him," she said. "I cannot just abandon him."

"If it is good enough for the princess to abandon her husband..." he said, referring to the current situation of the country's de facto queen, Princess Caroline, having separated from Prince George several years before.

"Oh, but everybody knew he was with Lady Jersey already when they married. He expected nothing from her."

"Well, to keep another person warm does not require that one lay her own body on the fire," he said, hoping to be encouraging.

Lady Rowereigh furrowed her brow but maintained a smile. "Lord Winthrope... you know that I feel very deeply for you. We are very good friends. But we cannot become any more than friends. What we have here is a beautiful illusion, which must one day be revealed for what it is."

"An illusion?" he said, an irked tone in his voice. His heart began to pound and an electric charge fueled by the flaming power of love ran through him. "So — this is an illusion?"

And he leaned in and planted a firm kiss upon her mouth. Agnes's heart raced with an electric combination of shock and passion. *Why?* She wondered in dismay, *Why did he have to do this?* Things had been going so well. This wasn't what she had wanted at all... except that in her heart, it really was. For a moment her own blood began to race and she leaned into the kiss, grasping his shoulder with her hand. For just a *moment* she could pretend.

When Lord Winthrope breathlessly pulled his face away from hers, their eyes met. There was a flash of confused looks, as each searched for answers in the eyes of the other.

"This... was a terrible idea," said Lord Winthrope, who knew too well the danger they were now in.

"Yes. A terrible idea," said Lady Rowereigh, her body shaking. She was not cold, but her nerves were so overwhelmed by what had just taken place that her body was forced into visceral effect. She cuddled up against him for support. Both turned their heads away from the other, ashamed of their own feelings, as they nestled their emotionally overtaxed figures closer together and their arms enwrapped each other. Lady Rowereigh was basically sitting on his lap.

"I suppose I had better go home now," said Lady Rowereigh, still not daring to look at him.

"Indeed," said he, staring at a collection of dust specks floating mid-room. "Would you — would you like to meet my sister tomorrow?"

"Your sister?" she answered with eyes fixed upon the wainscoting. "I suppose so. Yes. Will she be calling upon me?"

"If you would prefer that."

"It might be for the best," said she.

"As you like it."

Lady Rowereigh's nervous system was too stimulated by the force of her feelings, and her teeth were starting to chatter as she crawled off of Lord Winthrope so that he too could get up from the bench. As he stood, their eyes met again. Smiles crossed both their faces, as he led her out of the house, she still trembling. In perfect silence he escorted her back to her hotel, and only at the doorway did he bid her a customary farewell, and she likewise, both of them still smiling like idiots. He watched her disappear into the building.

Alas, the illusion was over. Things were getting real.

CHAPTER 8

Mrs. DeWitte finally had occasion to visit with Lord Winthrope for the first time since she had absconded at Heywood. She was almost certain that the woman with whom he was being seen around town was her own Agnes, but she felt she ought to inquire in order to be sure of it.

She paid a visit to him after breakfast on Tuesday, at his house, as everyone was well accustomed to overlook her doing. After the usual courtesies of greeting and necessary telling of how well Mr. DeWitte was or wasn't doing, she went in for the kill. "So, am I correct to hope that all proceeded well for you and Lady Rowereigh after I was forced to part your company?"

Winthrope replied in a friendly tone, "Forced, were you?"

"Oh, do not proceed upon it," she said with a laugh and a mocking of sincerity. "You know I was really very ill. So ill. And it was your good fortune that I was so, or no?"

"Oh, very good fortune," he answered.

"I am glad to hear it. Would it be impertinent of me to ask how it went?"

"The journey back was a trifle uneasy, after we had been deprived of your charming company," he answered, "but the troubles were overcome. As it happens, I am to introduce Lady Rowereigh to my sister this afternoon."

"Well, that is news! And is it Lady Rowereigh that has been seen in your company every day this passing week?"

His defensiveness was instinctual. "And what is the matter with that?"

"I myself am glad to hear it," answered Mrs. DeWitte. "Poor Agnes might become a bit of a scandal, however."

"I take it there is talk?"

"Naturally."

"Well, it would be wrong to say anything other than that she was my companion in public this week. We have done nothing to be ashamed of," he lied, figuring that the kiss needn't become known, even to Mrs. DeWitte.

"I will relay that. Still, you are in luck that her husband is such a terrible invalid, or you might have another duel to fight before the month is out. Did you hear that the surgeons had to cut off Sir Joshua's foot?"

"I had been informed of something to that effect," he answered, recalling the scene with Lady Hartley nearly two weeks ago.

"He has a sculptor carving a new foot out of wood for him. I cannot imagine how one should get it into a boot. One should think a simple, stuffed boot would be a more elegant solution!"

"But then he could not wear it to the balls," smirked Winthrope. And from there the conversation continued onto other subjects, with talk of Lady Rowereigh only coming up when Lord Winthrope invariably mentioned her and what he knew she had had to say about some particular subject, or how Lady Rowereigh had told him all about some notable thing, or how this topic reminded him so much of Lady Rowereigh — which was to say they ended up talking endlessly about Lady Rowereigh this and Lady Rowereigh that. At length, Lord Winthrope was forced to excuse himself, because the time had come to visit Lady Rowereigh and his sister Georgiana.

Mrs. DeWitte and Lord Winthrope said their goodbyes, and he set out at once for the short walk to the hotel where Agnes stayed. As Mrs. DeWitte climbed into her coach, looking off toward Winthrope being propelled to the house of his beloved, she could not help but wonder just what she had unleashed here.

At the hotel, Lord Winthrope waited in the front garden for his sister's arrival, that the two of them could go inside together to meet Agnes. Georgiana arrived in her phaeton — she lived in the Crescent up on the hill and across the river, which was enough of a journey that taking the horses between locations was not ridiculous for her. Her brother greeted her outside, and they went together into the building.

Lady Georgiana Murer had married a prosperous enough Baron that she got to live the life of luxury, with London seasons for the Parliament and Bath seasons for being away from horrid London, and plenty of balls and concerts and games to attend in either location. She passed a lot of time in stitching undergarments for the poor and making little tiny miniature paper cutouts. She presently had a small baby, who was being looked after by his nurse this afternoon. She was glad enough to get away from that — but she did wonder why, especially, her brother should have wanted her to meet this new woman? She did not know very much about her. Lionel had said only she was married — of course she was, or Lionel wouldn't be associating with her — and that she was a very dear friend who was visiting Bath for a water-cure.

When Agnes came forward to greet them, and looked upon Lionel, the immediate euphoria of the smile gained told Georgiana just what was going on. Lionel returned the same wide-eyed rush at the sight of Agnes. Georgiana was finding difficult in gaining any enthusiasm for her chance at being the third person in the room with them. Still, Lionel had never particularly introduced her to one of his married women before — was this some new ceremony he was going to be starting, or was there something special about Agnes?

Agnes had arranged hot chocolate to be served to her guests, from a special recipe that was really, mostly, a lot of brandy. She proudly pointed out that it was the brandy made from Winthrope's vineyards. Fanny passed out the cups to the group and Georgiana tried to conceal her disgust with the way that Agnes and Lionel were seated side by side and flirting and sitting together. It was not that she had any particular dislike for Agnes at this point, only that she felt the two lovebirds were really overdoing it and needed to get control of themselves. Were this not a new acquaintance she would have openly said as much.

"Well," said Georgiana, trying to be pleasant, "How have you two come to know each other?"

"Oh," answered Lionel, "a friend of ours introduced us at breakfast, one or two weeks ago."

"How pleasant. And, Lady Rowereigh, it is true you are here for a spa-cure?"

"That was my purpose… but really it is not for me, it is for my husband." The mention of the husband somewhat subdued Agnes's affections, for which Georgiana nearly cheered, because that meant at least now Lionel and Agnes were keeping their backsides to their own chairs.

"Is he at the baths now?" asked Georgiana. "Your husband, that is?"

"No, he has been too ill to travel, I was sent here to await him; I expect he shall arrive at any time now, for I have received no other word from him."

Georgiana wasn't sure whether to wish for the husband's arrival or not. "How pleasant," was all she could add in reply.

The visit was somewhat strained, from Lady Murer's viewpoint, and she was glad when it was finally over. It was possible that she might have gotten along with Agnes had they been conversing *tête-à-tête*, but with Lionel in the room making googly eyes the whole while, she had found the experience rather insufferable.

When Georgiana and Lionel had bid farewell to Agnes and left the hotel, Georgiana requested that her brother get into the phaeton with her and join her for a bit of a ride. Lionel agreed, and climbed in. Her footman rode behind on horseback.

As soon as they were out of earshot to anyone of importance, Georgiana spoke out. "I must beg you, Leo, to inform me of just what the point of all that had been?"

Lionel had been a bit too engrossed with Agnes to notice his sister's discomfort before this moment. It just now dawned on him that she might not have had a good time. "Oh. I am so sorry, was the visit not agreeable?" he said with a sinking feeling.

"It was like watching Italian actors mime out a love scene," she said with real aggravation.

Lionel bit his lip. He had hoped that Georgiana would just adore Agnes.

"I ask again," she said, her tone a little softened this time to suggest not so much annoyance but a genuine concern for her brother. "For I should like to know, what was it you had hoped to achieve by this?"

It was a good question, for even Lionel had not really given strong consideration to his motives. "I suppose," he replied, "I had harbored some hope that you should like one another. It simply seemed as if my sister and my w — " he stopped himself there, realizing what he was about to say.

"Your what?"

"My *dear friend*... that my sister and my dear friend should be acquainted, is all."

"You have never before introduced me to a 'dear friend' unless they were male and were to spend Christmas with us at the house. And you do not normally call your dear friend your *wife* or your *woman*," she said, having filled in his blank. But now she understood what was happening, at least. "You do not really expect to marry her, do you?"

Lionel was silent. The truth was that that *was* what his heart now desired from the relationship. He and Agnes could live in his townhouse there in Bath, and travel to London for the season, and visit the family home in Nottinghamshire for Christmas and Whitsuntide other such holidays... his sister's family would get along with her and make her feel welcome... they would have a nice respectable life... he wouldn't have to hang around with married women all the time because he had have one right at home... and even the happy DeWittes could never be as happy as they would surely be.

"Is her husband so sick as that?" asked Georgiana, wondering if maybe the man was at death's door and this marriage plan was more reasonable than it presently sounded.

"I know little enough about the absent husband, and if I am to be quite candid, I should like to keep it so." He really wished to prevent himself any grounded thoughts about the man who had the right to dictate Agnes's comings and goings and put his hands all over her whenever he might want. Keeping him as an abstract shadow — an invisible worm — was as much as he could take.

Georgiana gave her brother a heartfelt smile. "I know I have no influence over your actions here; I can only hope it turns out well for you." Realistically, though, she felt this was going to either culminate in a sinister murder, a scandalous divorce, or a stunning heartbreak for her brother. She knew enough of her brother to understand that when he had a passion for something, be it poetry or love, there was no hope of interfering, no hope of turning him back; and his seeming carelessness for society was in fact his reaction to the innumerable disappointments his too-strong passion had been forced to endure.

Georgiana deposited Lionel back at his house, then drove her phaeton onward to her own place, with her footman trotting alongside. As soon as she got home she met her husband and began to complain to him about the ridiculous visit, and told every detail she could — this was not with any deliberate idea to spread gossip or incriminate her brother, she simply had a tendency to air her grief to her spouse and vaguely expected that it was safe to do so. But then, when Lord Murer went to his club that night, he made a small mention of the affair when somebody inquired after his wife. And meanwhile that following footman, who had overheard everything, was blabbing to all the other servants about it: and in Bath, the social classes tended to mix a little more than they did in some other realms, which meant that within a few days pretty much everyone in town knew about Lord Winthrope and his fanatical devotion to Lady Rowereigh, who was the wife of a Sir Howard Rowereigh. The classy people tried not to be judgmental about it; but all the same, the sight of Lady Rowereigh and Lord Winthrope together was no longer overlooked by the public.

CHAPTER 9

Agnes was just finishing her breakfast, alone in her rooms, when there was a knock at her door. She hoped that it might be an announcement that Lord Winthrope had come to visit — which he usually did around this time of day. She opened, but instead was informed by the porter that she had received a letter from Sir Howard, and was presented with it. Her husband's stamp was immediately recognizable on the wax seal. She paid for the postage, and took it inside.

Standing alone in her parlour, Agnes held the letter her her hands, but was afraid to open it. It was very likely to be an announcement that he was departing for Bath and was perhaps one or two days behind the note. What would become of she and Lord Winthrope then? Of course they hadn't done anything indecent — well, apart from that kiss, and maybe sitting too closely together, okay okay, *cuddling* — and certainly being just two good friends shouldn't compel any reason to worry over the return of her husband, right? She groaned at the thought — she could not deceive even herself with the lie, at this point; and if she no longer believed, how could she expect to convince anyone else of her innocence?

Bravely she opened the letter, and discovered that the news was not at all what she expected. Sir Howard would not be coming at all! And furthermore, he had given her permission to remain in Bath for as long as she deemed fit! *This was practically a gift from God.* Why, she could keep on with Lord Winthrope for weeks if she wanted!

She pictured delivering the good news to Winthrope. How happy they would be! And without fear of her husband bursting in at any moment, maybe they could even... no. *No.* She was still married. And she would have to return to Sir Howard eventually. When she did, she wanted to be able to look him in the face and say with perfect honesty that she had been faithful to him.

She started to think it over. How long could she keep this up? Though her husband had given her permission to stay in Bath, his words hinted that he expected her back eventually. How long could she stretch it out for? 12 weeks, maybe? What then? She would have to leave Lord Winthrope. There was no other way — unless Howard did change his mind and come out to Bath. That wouldn't be much better. She closed her eyes and thought hard. What was the best possible, realistic outcome of all this? All she could see were two possible roads: a perfect, happy future with Lord Winthrope, which she knew was unsustainable, or the necessary return to her husband, bleak and dismal as it was.

Tears began forming in Agnes's eyes. How much longer could she pretend? Even if she delayed the departure from Bath, what could she gain by it? The longer she stayed with Lord Winthrope, the greater the danger that she would be tempted to violate her marriage vows. And the longer she stayed, the harder the final separation would become — and it *would* become.

She tried to console herself with thoughts that perhaps, Lord Winthrope could journey out to visit her at the castle — just as friends, and they could still see each other from time to time, and draw things out a little longer and not have to sever their relationship entirely. But no. She realized that not only could such an arrangement never be satisfying, but that she did not want him to observe her in the wretched ruins of her home, that dark place, with foul air, cold walls and all her life devoted to Howard. Their thoughts of one another should remain pure: they should stay happy thoughts of their vibrant times in Bath.

She sunk her head into her hands and began to cry. There was no way out: the time had come to return home to her husband, and to bid farewell to Lord Winthrope and all her beautiful dreams of the future.

Elsewhere in town, Lionel was entirely unaware of the catastrophe which had struck his beloved Agnes. He was smilingly planning to see her that afternoon, thinking out the details of what the day's entertainment might be. He had, however, become aware of the notice that the public were giving to the relationship. While he was confident that he himself had nothing to fear as far as scandal, he desired not to subject Agnes to rumors or any loss of reputation, and so he was trying to delay his usual visit to her for as long as he could, for the sake of decency, so that people would not be wondering if his presence with her in the morning might not mean he had been with her all night. For now he was at the Parade coffee-house, and he took in the famous view of the landscape from the location; for the Parade coffee-house was said to be the most pleasant coffee-house in all of England. He sipped at sugary cups of black liquid while reading newspapers that talked of how horrible it was that the Prince of Wales had abandoned his own wife.

After stretching out his breakfast for as long as he could stand, he tried to take a nice long walk along the river to pass a little more time. As he strolled, he caught sight of Lady Hartley, walking alongside her husband Sir Joshua, who was pushed in an invalid-chair by a servant. His lower legs were covered by a blanket so that one might not immediately notice his missing foot.

Supposedly, a duel meant that the matter was thereafter settled and everyone's honor was satisfied. It was expected that the incident was not to be brought up again. However, the malevolent glare Lord Winthrope received, from both the Hartleys as he passed them, well indicated he was not truly forgiven and forgotten.

As he continued to stroll along, Lionel noticed the fresh open skies of Bath starting to close in with dark clouds. A storm was on its way.

Behind him, once certain he had passed from earshot, the Hartleys began to talk.

"Such a bold-faced creature!" cried Sir Joshua, reducing his cries to a whispered volume. "To think he would even show his face in this town again!"

"I hear he is with a new married woman, the wife of some knight or baronet," answered

Lady Hartley. "Though you must have frightened him to some degree, for what I hear, is he takes precautions this time — he has chosen a lady whose husband is left in the country somewhere, so there is nobody to challenge him."

Hartley let out a snorting sort of laugh. "The coward! Such pretensions of honor, but has not a thread of it to back himself. Some good person ought to alert that husband, and perhaps this time it should be Lord Winthrope who loses his foot."

Lady Hartley was struck with an idea. "The mail-coaches leave from the White Hart Inn, not far from here. I do not know the husband's name... but the White Hart is directly across from the Pump Rooms, and certainly people there would have some idea."

The couple proceeded at once to the Pump Room, on pretence of taking the waters, and began chit-chatting with some friends and acquaintances who were promenading. Lady Hartley, who was a smart woman, was able to twist the conversation toward the gossip about Lord Winthrope and that new friend of his, oh what's her name, oh yes, as you say, Lady Rowereigh. What is her husband again, a Baron? A baronet. Oh no, I simply imagined for a moment he might have been somebody I met several years ago at a dinner. Unless he is the one who lives in Cheshire? Ah — the one from the rotten borough of Goseth Tree, yes I remember, and it is Lord Haversham over there who reaped the rewards of that deal! Oh please do forgive me, if that is Lord Haversham I absolutely must go over and say good-morning to him.

Within an hour, Lady Hartley had pried up all the information she needed to be enabled to write a letter to Sir Howard and send it to his noble home in the vicinity of Yorkshire. The powdered footmen at White Hart were happy to provide paper, ink and wax to the Hartleys *gratis* in consideration of a very large tip. A short note was written alerting Sir Howard that his wife was enjoying herself in Bath too much with the infamous Viscount Winthrope, and that for the sake of decency, and the future of the Rowereigh line, it must be stopped. Sounded good enough. Lord Hartley folded and sealed the note, then addressed it to Sir Howard Rowereigh, Bart., Castle Rowereigh, Yorkshire. They handed it off to a footman, with another penny tip, and watched from the windows of the White Hart as the note was deposited into the mail-coach headed for the midlands.

And across the river, wholly unaware of what had happened at two sides of town that morning, Lord Winthrope presented himself at the Sydney hotel, expecting to visit with Agnes. He was permitted entry as was customary, and he bore the customary smile on his face. But when he saw Agnes in person, all the cheer left him: something was wrong. She came forward looking puffy and pale, like she had been crying, and there was not a happy expression upon her face to greet him.

"Please have a seat, Lord Winthrope," she said with a chilling formality.

Winthrope sat, but looked upon his beloved Agnes with the greatest concern. "I cannot help but think there is something the matter, Agnes," he said without thinking. The mistake was recognized at once and he felt a powerful sting of humiliation for the breach of etiquette he had just made by addressing her so. He could see Agnes wince at it, too. He hurried to finish his thought. "Please, *Lady Rowereigh*, if there is any way I can relieve you..."

"Something is the matter," she answered, not looking at him. She politely took a seat across from him, but could bring herself to make no eye contact. She knew that if she looked at him, only two things could happen: either her heart would break, and she would be sent into fits of sobbing and wailing that would surely draw the servants and end the conversation before it could even begin; or else her heart would melt, and she would be unable to do what was necessary, but rather be instantly drawn back into the waiting arms of her Lord Winthrope and to the life of love and happiness that was not meant for her. "Winthrope..." she said. Her body felt like it was frozen with ice.

Winthrope's heart ached painfully. "Agnes..." he said again, this time without fear.

"Lord Winthrope, I must return home to my husband," she blurted out as rapidly as she could. Her body trembled, but she was proud of herself for at least getting that far.

And what could Lionel say to that? He knew he had no right to object to it.

There was a long silence, several minutes, as the two sat across from one another, neither daring to look the other in the face. Neither was certain if there was anything more worth saying, even though their hearts were full of all the things they *wished* to express. Tears began to bead up in the eyes of Lord Winthrope, as he imagined a last-ditch all-or-nothing move of throwing himself at her feet and begging that she abandon her husband and marry him instead — they could move to France or the Netherlands or some other place where no one would care who they were — that there was no reason to sacrifice her happiness for the sake of duty — and he imagined her delightful agreement, an agreement which he knew would never really come, because in some way, everyone had to sacrifice happiness for the sake of duty. The duels he fought, the glares from women who felt wronged, those were the prices he was paying. To him they were nothing; he had wealth, status and power to console him for his losses. But Agnes, he knew full well, had nothing but that invisible worm, that awful husband, and if she went against society she would lose her family, she would lose her status, and even if he became her protector and the two of them hid away together in France or the Netherlands, then what? There was no civilized country on earth where two people of their position could behave in such a way and yet be respected.

"I shall show myself out," he said mechanically, breaking the silence at last.

Agnes choked back tears as she listened to the rustling of silk as he rose, then the leather on wood as his feet took him to the door, and the brass handle which clicked as he turned it.

"Goodbye, Lady Rowereigh," said he. And he was gone.

The second that he left the room, Agnes let out a wail that could be heard several rooms over, and her eyes burst into tears enough to fill the Avon.

And Lord Winthrope himself scarcely made it the half-mile home, and as he traveled he bore upon him a look of such severe distress that he was twice stopped on the street by people asking whether he was alright, which he had to quickly grunt off. When he got through his own front door, he too collapsed into a fit of weeping and swooning that would have disgusted him to have witnessed.

CHAPTER 10

Agnes spent a terrible day and night in weeping, after which her chest ached and her head felt like it would burst. She could not bear the sight of food, and her servants were not able to provide her with any comfort. Six weeks of spa treatments were undone in an evening: by the next morning she looked as withered and defeated as she had before Harrogate.

She was not even certain whether she could make the trip home in her current state. And so, hoping to have something to show for all her time spent in Bath, she had her coachman drive her down to the King's Baths early in the morning, to be one of the day's first users of the tub. The hot waters helped to soothe the freezing ache in her chest and to put a little color back into her face.

By breakfast time, she was just able to stomach some buttered Bath buns, and she ordered Fanny to go to the bakery from which they had been delivered, with instructions to collect the recipe so it might be used back at home.

Then she sat down and composed a letter to her husband, informing him that as he was no longer expected in Bath, she herself had no more reason to remain, and that she would be departing the city before the weekend to return home. She signed the letter 'Your dutiful wife' and paid a footman of the hotel to deposit it upon the next mail-coach. She followed it by composing another note to Susannah DeWitte, bidding farewell and thanking her for her kindness and attention, and giving a courtesy invitation to visit her in the midlands, which she knew she would never invoke. This she sent with a footman to be presented directly.

She thought about sending a letter to Lord Winthrope, but decided against it.

And as she had nothing else to do in the afternoon, and she couldn't bear the thought of going to see anymore of the attractions that she had enjoyed with Lord Winthrope, she simply poured herself a tall glass of brandy, drank it all, and went to sleep, free from the miseries of her feelings. And when she awoke after dark she had some more brandy, and returned to her slumber, without giving a thought about dinner.

The next morning she made a final trip to the King's Baths, soaked till she was wrinkled, then returned to the hotel where she told Fanny to begin packing for their journey home. They departed in the afternoon, and got as far as Castle Combe before retiring at a small inn for the night.

When, five days later, she and the servants arrived back at the dark and danky Rowereigh Castle, she was very astounded to learn that Sir Howard was not there.

In Bath, the weather was rainy and the skies were dark. It had been a stormy week. As the little light that filtered through the clouds began to vanish, Lord Winthrope sat in his library, a hot toddy by his side and a lamp of whale-oil burning before him, as he endeavored to brighten his spirits by losing himself in the antics of Humphrey Clinker or The Grubthorpe Family; but he could never seem to concentrate for more than a few pages, and none of the humor was satisfying him. His heart was suffering, and there was no relief in existence: his brain could focus on nothing but Agnes, and the torment of her absence. After hours of trying, he was ready to abandon the project of seeking good cheer, and to try to find consolation instead in the woeful pages of Ossian. Just as he opened the pages to start reading, a visitor was announced. Winthrope was actually relieved.

"A visitor? Who is it?" he asked of his porter.

The porter answered all too casually: "He introduced himself as Sir Howard Rowereigh."

Winthrope's eyes went wide with shock. His heart sank and he struggled to maintain an icy composure. "Well. Well then... I suppose you shall have to show him in," he responded flatly. The servant went out immediately to collect the visitor. Winthrope, alone, staggered backwards and had to support himself against the library wall to keep from collapsing, as it seemed like the very beating of his heart had ceased. Sir Howard! Here! This was too much for his already-wounded soul. What could Sir Howard possibly want? He began to wonder if Agnes had called for her husband, but couldn't imagine why she should have; especially since he knew she had already left the city. Had the husband found them out? But how?

A tall, shadowy figure entered the library doorway. Winthrope had never particularly visualized Howard Rowereigh, but had always vaguely imagined him as a short, fat, bald man of at least fifty years: some unattractive nuisance, a man who had no right to claim such a creature as Agnes for his own. But now, before him, was a very different picture: a sickly but frankly very handsome gentleman, tall, lean, strikingly pale, dark circles round his dark eyes, his long bushy hair hanging limp as beads of water dripped from the strands. He was barely ten years older than Lord Winthrope. He was soaking wet from the rain; the servants had taken his overcoat, but the water had already penetrated to his dark colored suit, turning it a blackish-hue. On his hip he carried a silver sword, and a flask of medicine. The look upon the man's face was a mixture of anguish and outrage, but borne with a dignity that Winthrope would not have expected from a mere country baronet.

Rowereigh leaned against the doorway the same way Winthrope leaned against the wall: each was just on the verge of collapse. Gradually, Winthrope came to realize this, recovered himself, and invited his guest to have a seat with all the customary respect a guest was due. Rowereigh threw himself into a chair with a muttered thank you.

Winthrope was no stranger to dealing with offended husbands, but typically the husbands had nothing whatsoever about which to be rightly offended. This case was a little different, for though he and Agnes had never committed any technical definition of *adultery*, they certainly had crossed more than a few lines of propriety; and he absolutely wanted to protect Agnes (wherever could she be?) against her husband's wrath. This left him somewhat at a loss for action.

"You are the Viscount Winthrope?" asked Rowereigh with a tinge of aggression.

"Indeed," answered Winthrope. "How may I be of service?"

"I have received this note, which has brought me no small amount of concern," said Rowereigh, as he produced it from his pocket. "It is unsigned, but it makes some particular accusations against my wife, and against you." He handed the letter to Winthrope, who read it over and read as much.

Winthrope took a deep breath. "I do apologize that such a concerning letter did reach you. The truth is that I am acquainted with your wife, or was, while she was in Bath."

"She is not here?"

"She returned to you several days ago, or said she would," said Winthrope, whose voice betrayed a sincere mystification and concern for her safety.

"I received the note about six days ago, and proceeded here with utmost haste." Rowereigh's face seemed to be growing a little flushed, and his breathing was growing heavy. "It may be possible we missed each other."

"In any event," continued Winthrope, "your wife did nothing to offend you. It is true that I became enamored of her, and sought to pursue her; I had tricked her into spending a few hours in my company, but when she realized my intentions, she barred me from further contact, and left the city. Anything said to the contrary would be vile gossip. Whoever wrote this note," he said, holding it up, "must surely have been some jealous lady or a nosey prankster, seeking to stir up trouble."

Rowereigh leaned his head back, eyes closed painfully, and nodded as if his mind were really elsewhere. There was a pause, in which he took a slow, deep breath, and after which he said very curtly, "Do you really expect me to believe that load of bollocks?"

Winthrope was surprised; but then he realized that in all his imaginings of Rowereigh, he had been mistaken. An unattractive, selfish, stupid fellow like he had envisioned would have never won the hand of a girl like Agnes! He couldn't treat this man like some bug who could be brushed away. A disinterested man might have been glad for the convenient story, but this was a person who was genuinely desirous of defending what was his.

Suddenly Sir Howard started. He pulled a handkerchief from his pocket which he desperately used to cover his mouth. Winthrope watched him with alarm.

"Sir, are you alright?"

Rowereigh heaved his body a couple of times. His stomach was empty — he had had no food all that day — but he still vomited a smattering of bile into the cloth. When he was done, he folded the handkerchief away, trembling, and looked at Winthrope with apologetic eyes. "Forgive me. I have not been well, for some time."

Winthrope's face softened. He found that he felt a genuine pathos for this man: intelligent, handsome, quite in love — and dreadfully ill.

"...But the matter at hand," Rowereigh insisted, "is my wife, Lady Rowereigh. Had you said you did not know her at all, I might believe some mere prankster had been looking for a laugh at my expense — but nobody composes a letter like that over a failed seduction."

Winthrope was feeling a great strain. Head in hands, he sank down onto the bench in the library, facing Rowereigh. "It is true," said Winthrope, looking up at his rival, "that I have exaggerated her fidelity — but not by much. I did not need to trick her into spending time with me, and we enjoyed each other's company. We spent a few evenings here in this very library, reading poetry. She spoke of you often; she was anticipating your visit to Bath with much delight; but she had nothing else to occupy her while she awaited you. We were introduced by a female friend; and it fell to me to entertain her with conversations, card games, sports, music — the entertainments of this city. For, what man could stand to see her looking so weary and miserable, wandering the streets all alone, preparing for this husband who she was certain would appear any day — and now appears only after she has left?"

"One expects fidelity from his wife," said Rowereigh, "and that she will not falter."

"You can be assured that I have never injured you, and, to all my knowledge, neither has she. She has been gay, but not unfaithful." Winthrope rose, puffed his chest forward, and folded his hands behind his back as he added, "And I would stake my life on that statement."

Rowereigh smirked briefly, imagining the chance to spill blood, before the pall of reality conquered his thoughts. "Ah, no," he said. "If I were in better health, I am sure I would demand satisfaction. But I am frail, I can barely stand up anymore... and I have no faith in spa waters to save me," he added bitterly.

"Then," said Winthrope, "Let us be friends, and have no jealousies against one another. Lady Rowereigh came to me in consideration of you, and left me in consideration of you. Her choice is apparent. Return to your Agnes —" Winthrope could feel the sting of tears trying to break past his eyes, but did his utmost to restrain them " — and make her happy."

Rowereigh could see the sincerity of the man's words reflected in his face, and his heart broke. He wondered if he himself had perhaps reached the apex of suffering — his painfully bad health rendering him so useless, his dutiful wife staying by his side even though it seemed to be killing her. He trusted Lord Winthrope was telling the truth now, and Rowereigh found it was bringing him every bit as much pain as would have news that she had abandoned him. What was the good in keeping Agnes if he didn't have the power to enjoy her presence? What good was her love and devotion if he was perpetually in an opium haze and knew not what happened around him? All he was doing was destroying her happiness and bringing her down to his own wretched level. *Solamen miseris socios habuisse doloris*, as the devil said to Faustus.

Rowereigh began to stand up, intending to bid farewell to his host, but the movement proved too much for his weak organs and it threw him into another heave, albeit with nothing left inside him to come out. He crumpled back down to the floor and choked for a moment, his body still trying to expel poisons that it could never be rid of.

Winthrope approached him in concern and knelt down with him on the floor. "You are unwell. Should you like me to call for a doctor?"

"I do not believe a doctor will be any service, for not a one has helped me these six months last," gasped Rowereigh. His teeth began to chatter in pain as his organs seemed to be twisting in upon themselves.

"Well, then, you must allow me at least to see you to your rooms?"

"I have not yet taken any rooms," Rowereigh managed to say through clenched teeth. "My first business upon entering Bath, was to locate you."

"Then you must allow me to make some arrangements for you. Please, wait here while I send my man ahead of you."

"If you would assist me back into the chair..."

"Of course."

Winthrope helped his visitor over to the bench, where he could lie down if needed. Rowereigh, once secured, removed the flask of laudanum from his hip, and took a mouthful. "This will have some effect in a few minutes..." he said, trying to save whatever face he had left. "I had missed my dose this evening…"

"Please sit here, and I will return presently."

Winthrope hurried out of the room to send his servants for lodging, coaches and doctors. He was gone for several minutes, during which time Rowereigh noticed a copy of the poems of Ossian sitting nearby, and automatically began to peruse it.

It is night. I am alone, forlorn on the hill of storms. The wind is heard in the mountain. The torrent shrieks down the rock. No hut receives me from the rain, forlorn on the hill of winds. Rise, moon, from behind thy clouds; stars of the night appear! Lead me, some light, to the place where my love rests from the toil of the chase, his bow near him, unstrung, his dogs panting around him. But here I must sit alone, by the rock of the mossy stream. The stream and the wind roar; nor can I hear the voice of my love.

Why delays my Salgar, why the son of the hill, his promise? Here is the rock, and the tree; and here the roaring stream. Thou didst promise with night to be here. Ah! Whither is my Salgar gone? With thee I would fly, my father; with thee, my brother of pride. Our race have long been foes; but we are not foes, O Salgar!

I sit in my grief. I wait for morning in my tears. Rear the tomb, ye friends of the dead; but close it not till Colma come. My life flies away like a dream: why should I stay behind? Here shall I rest with my friends, by the stream of the sounding rock. When night comes on the hill; when the wind is on the heath; my ghost shall stand in the wind, and mourn the death of my friends. The hunter shall hear from his booth. He shall fear but love my voice. For sweet shall my voice be for my friends; for pleasant were they both to me.

The woes of the ancient bards and warriors struck him as meager, compared to his own unhappiness; the descriptions too vague to be true outpourings of pain and shame. His own grief was so strong he felt he needed a stronger dose of the laudanum, and took a second swig.

He thought of Agnes, and how unhappy he had made her.

He thought of poor Frances, whose life he had cut short because she displeased him.

And he thought of his beloved Laura, long dead, and the only one he had ever found any happiness with.

And he took another drink of laudanum, and then another drink of laudanum, and then another...

CHAPTER 11

Agnes stood in her childhood church, the same place where she had been married. The building had been much the same for hundreds of years: same cold stone walls, same stained glasses, same wooden retable at the altar. The one thing that sometimes changed was the number of dead interred within the church — a new stone monument would sometimes appear to mark the latest permanent resident of the holy building.

Now she stood before a freshly cut block of granite that was fixed into the wall, which read:

BELOW THIS STONE REST THE MORTAL REMAINS OF
SIR HOWARD ROWEREIGH (GRIMESBY), BART.
BORN DECEMBER 21ST, 1769 AT GOSETH TREE
DIED SEPTEMBER 1ST, 1810 AT BATH
IN PACE REQUIESCAT

It was followed by a large blank space where her own details were expected to go one day.

Having no heirs, the title of Baronet Rowereigh was to be dissolved. She had moved out of the dreadful Castle Rowereigh at once, with its dark, crumbling rooms and unhappy memories, and was residing again with her parents.

Of course she had inherited her share of the Rowereigh fortune and property — the nouveau-riche family had not been sophisticated enough to put any sort of entail on it, and the marriage contract had specified she be comfortably provided for if she outlived her spouse. She didn't really care too much for the fortune, although it did bring her some delight to help out her poor parents with gifts and financial assistance for their old age: she had bought them a new house in the country and arranged an annuity for them. Many of Rowereigh's servants had moved over to their household, easing the burdens on poor old Ginny as well. But Agnes herself didn't have much use for the money, as far as she was concerned — she had been raised frugally, and never really acquired any particularly expensive habits during her short married life. She had paid off the creditors for her trip to Bath at the same time she paid off her husband's funeral expenses.

To the best of her knowledge, her husband had changed his mind about traveling to Bath sometime after writing the letter to say he wasn't coming — why the change, she could only guess — and shortly after booking himself into the the same hotel where she had been staying, he became very ill, and after a few days of unconsciousness, passed from the world. The medical men had bled him and done all else they could for his cure, but to no avail. It was one of these kind medical men, Mr. Hutchinson, who taken the task upon himself to notify Lady Rowereigh of Sir Howard's fate. A sympathetic patron — some friend of Sir Howard's in Bath, no doubt — had paid the expense of shipping the body back to his home in the midlands, and it was Mr. Hutchinson who attended the corpse on his journey and at length informed the new widow of what had occurred.

She did not know about the Hartley's letter, the confrontation between Rowereigh and Winthrope, the intentional overdose of laudanum, or that it was Lord Winthrope who dutifully made the final arrangements for Sir Howard out of respect to the man's wife.

A few months had passed — she had been widowed now for almost as long as she had been married. Her ugly wardrobe had all been dyed black, which was no harm to it. And now that she was a wealthy, young widow, suitors were coming out of the woodwork for her — and the bit of reputation she had acquired in Bath was making her especially desirable to a certain type of gentleman, a type very unlike Sir Howard. There was even a lecherous old Duke who had come snooping after her, hoping to attract a third wife to look after his large brood. Agnes was utterly cool to their attentions, for she was not very interested in a remarriage. How could she be? What good had marriage done her but ruin her health and peace of mind? What good had love done for her but to pierce her with the indescribable suffering of its absence? Even the money she had won from the adventure, seemed to her like a bad trade. In effect, through the split with Lord Winthrope and the death of her husband, she had lost her two great loves in one week, and that was a pain from which it was going to take time to recover.

She still thought often of Lord Winthrope — too much she thought of him, really. He was always the first thought she had upon waking in the morning. Sometimes, while engrossed in some activity, she found herself muttering his name for no apparent reason at all. She wished that she could confide in him all the strange things that had been happening in her life lately. He would probably have something sarcastic to say about the new suitors, or some good advice that she wouldn't take. In light of how it all turned out, she sometimes wondered if she ought to have listened when he suggested that she should separate from her husband and abscond with him — but it did not matter now. What was done was done.

Feeling guilty that, even in visiting the grave of her husband, so many of her thoughts were toward another man, she deposited the bouquet she had fashioned from tiny wildflowers, and hurried out of the church. It was an important day to have paid such a visit: it was the one year anniversary of their marriage in that same building.

When she arrived back at her parent's home, she discovered that there was a package waiting for her, delivered by the mail-coach that morning. It was a large bundle wrapped in cloth, and seemed to have more cloth within. She untied the securing strings, and found the wrapper had been concealing six cheerfully colored gowns, cut in the new Gothic style. She was initially perplexed by them, but then she came to realize

— these were the gowns she had ordered in Bath last year! She had completely forgotten about them. Evidently it took a few months for the dressmaker to figure out where he should send them. How convenient that one could send things all over the country by mail!

The idea of the mail sat vaguely in her mind all through dinner that evening, as did the recollections of her fond time at Bath. By morning, she had convinced herself to compose a letter:

My dear Lord Winthrope,

I hope you shall not think it brash of me to write to you. If you do, please read no further and discard this letter at once.

I have been suffering with much regret for the way I conducted myself in Bath last year. Not for my breach of the rules of society, which I am sure I have abused to no small regard, but rather for how I treated you and others for whom I cared so deeply. I shall be forever grateful for the kindness shown to me by

Susannah DeWitte, though I have said so few words to her in my life that such kindness shown by her bewilders me. To your sister I should like to extend my deepest apologies for my conduct (and yours!) during her visit. And to you, my dear friend, I cannot communicate the sorrows which burden my heart for the circumstances of our parting! I often feel that I should have written to you sooner than this, to thank you for your kindness to me. I often reflect upon the poems we read together, and our idle talks, and I hold back tears for the loss of them.

I do not suppose it would be known to you, but my husband has died. He left us some months ago, about the time that I returned from Bath. That was a strange and unhappy circumstance, though which I will be glad to unbosom to you if you are willing to write me again in the future.

I hope that the bitterness of our parting does not resound too strongly in your heart and that you can forgive me for any grief I may have caused you.

Your friend, Agnes Rowereigh

She blew the ink dry, then folded the letter. Staring at the back of it, she realized that she was unsure as to just where it should be mailed. To Bath? She knew his address there, but it was Parliament season — he might be in London this time of year.

The letter sat unmailed for several days as she tried to learn through her limited means just where the note should be sent in order for Lord Winthrope to receive it. She could learn nothing, it seemed; and in time the letter was forgotten altogether.

Months passed, spring came into full bloom, then settled into the rainy heat of summer. Agnes passed the time comfortably with her parents; she sewed shirts for the poor, and had begun to make an effort to read more poetry, whenever she could. Suitors came, sometimes pursued her for a few weeks, but always left in dismay.

Then in July, Agnes received a letter. It was from Susannah DeWitte. The cheerful letter, so characteristic of Mrs. DeWitte, recalled the fond times had in Bath the previous year, hoped for many more bright days to come, and invited Agnes to visit her again in the summer, in that same city.

And Agnes, feeling like she had been in mourning long enough and could use a little good cheer, packed her colorful Gothic gowns and with Fanny again in tow, made the journey for Bath.

In the city, Agnes took fine lodgings, wore her fine gowns, and felt like a fine woman. The fresh stone buildings looked bright and welcoming, the sunny southern skies radiated joy. She called upon the DeWittes, and there were smiles all around.

The morning after her first day, the DeWittes invited her to the public breakfast in the gardens. The group were sitting cheerfully and discussing pleasant topics, when Mrs. DeWitte somewhat importunely brought up the unhappy matter of Lord Winthrope.

"Have you heard anything about him?" she asked, with a smile that failed to allow one to think badly of it.

"I?" said Agnes. "No, I have known nothing of him since my leaving Bath last year. I am not even aware if he is still in the city or not."

"Oh, I think he is within the city," said Mrs. DeWitte, her eyes gleaming.

Agnes was somewhat terrified by the thought of seeing him again, after the unhappy parting they'd had. Could he forgive her? Could they still like each other? She felt like she should just let it rest as a happy memory and try to avoid any future with him. "Well, unless I have cause to encounter him in public, I do not suppose I will be seeing anymore of him."

Mrs. DeWitte made a spinning gesture with the index finger of her hand. When Agnes seemed not to respond immediately, she did it again. Agnes was seeing the gesture but not understanding it. Still smiling, but with a tone of slight annoyance now, Mrs. DeWitte leaned forward and muttered to the ignorant Agnes: "He just sat down behind you."

Agnes turned automatically, and her eyes were met by those of Lord Winthrope.

Winthrope had come to the breakfast in the company of a different party, but their table happened to be put right beside that of the DeWittes. He had recognized the women's voices and turned around to try to identify them just at the same time that Agnes had twisted round.

The couple stared into one another's eyes for just a brief moment before simultaneously jumping back in their seats, as if they'd each been hit with a shock of electricity. Then they at once were seized with emotion and turned back toward each other. Propriety did not matter now.

"Lord Winthrope —"

"Lady Rowereigh — I did not know you had returned to Bath — "

"I came in only yesterday."

Lord Winthrope rose to his feet. Lady Rowereigh's apprehensions, about meeting him again, seemed to have vanished entirely.

The bond between their two souls was strong as ever, and had needed only a catalyst to bring them back into an active state. There were no thoughts of the unhappy past or regrettable behaviors — only the explosive joy they now felt at seeing each other again.

Winthrope's party made no objection to Lady Rowereigh and her party commuting over to their table; they could see how delighted their friend was to have Lady Rowereigh in his presence again. Winthrope and his lady sat side by side and barely showed interest in breakfast from that point on. They let out such a sparkling energy that they became the talk of the whole table, and there was a group-wide excitement for the reunited lovers.

And that night, the couple were seen by a few people on the street going into Lord Winthrope's house; and there were a few people who saw them emerge again, together, the next morning. It was viewed as significant that some of Winthrope's servants were sent out subsequently to purchase a new bed from a cabinetmaker, as evidently there had been some kind of sudden destruction of the old one.

On the following day, Lord Winthrope purchased a Common License and he and Agnes were married the day after that, in a very small ceremony, with Mr. and Mrs. DeWitte bearing witness. Of course Agnes was then obliged to write to her parents and suddenly explain *that*; but she was a widow over 21 years of age and had every right to marry whomever and whenever she wanted. She had served her time, and freedom now was hers.

After a couple weeks had passed, and all the world had wrapped their heads around the sudden marriage of the Viscount Winthrope to the widow of Sir Howard, the vibrant young couple sat together in what was now their own home. They could now be Agnes and Lionel with one another, come and go with one another as they pleased, and not give a toss about what the world thought of them; for with their marriage — this small consideration to the ways of the world — they had gained their freedom. Such was the price they had to pay, but at last it was a worthy price.

END.